D0927941

Wind Over Rimfire

Wind Over Rimfire

WAYNE C. LEE

Sagebrush
Large Print Westerns

Library of Congress Cataloging in Publication Data

Lee, Wayne C.
    Wind over Rimfire / Wayne C. Lee.
        p.   cm.
    ISBN 1-57490-046-3 (hc : alk. paper)
    1. Western stories. 2. Large type books. I. Title
[PS3523.E34457W56   1996]
813'.54--dc20   96-42252
                                                                    CIP

Cataloguing in Publication Data is available from
the British Library and the National Library of Australia.

Sagebrush Large Print Westerns are published in the
United States and Canada by Thomas T. Beeler, Publisher,
Box 659, Hampton Falls, New Hampshire 03844-0659.
ISBN 1-57490-046-3

Published in the United Kingdom, Eire, and the Republic of
South Africa by Isis Publishing Ltd, 7 Centremead, Osney
Mead, Oxford OX2 0ES England. ISBN 0-7531-5180-4

Published in Australia and New Zealand by Australian
Large Print Audio & Video Pty Ltd, 17 Mohr Street,
Tullamarine, Victoria, 3043, Australia. ISBN 1-86340-676-X

Manufactured in the United States of America

CHAPTER I

He rode into the unsuspecting town of Rimfire from the south on a soft balmy morning in late April. Reed Coleman stood in the doorway of the marshal's office and watched him come like an evil wind springing up out of the badlands.

As Reed moved out on the porch for a better view, the light from the street reflected off the star on his vest. Even at that distance, Reed recognized the man for what he was. He had hoped he would never see a man like that in this town.

The man didn't go directly to the saloon, as a thirsty traveler might have been expected to do. Instead, he reined up at the hotel, swung down and went inside. The hotel was almost a block down the street from the marshal's office, but Reed, studying the man carefully, noted the holster that rode low on the man's thigh. It didn't slide around when he dismounted, a sure sign that it was tied down. Other things about the way the man moved, never taking his hand far from his holster even while he was dismounting, clearly indicated his reliance on the gun. Reed waited for the man to reappear. He was probably just passing through. Men like that found nothing worth stopping for in Rimfire. Still, Reed was uneasy. Why had he gone to the hotel instead of the saloon? There was nothing at the hotel in mid-morning for a traveler not planning to stay awhile.

Running his eyes up and down the quiet street, Reed tried to calm his uneasiness. Rimfire was as peaceful a town as ever sprang out of the prairie west of the Missouri. Trouble didn't come there because there was nothing for it to feed on. Reed's job as marshal was little more than a title.

1

It meant more to Reed than that, however, for he drew a salary, and he had a place for every penny. He thought of the little piece of land he had bought, but he didn't have money enough to buy cattle to stock it. Thoughts of the ranch he hoped to build turned his eyes automatically toward the schoolhouse over in the southwest part of town where Martha Preston would be giving arithmetic lessons to the town's youngsters about now.

He couldn't see the schoolhouse because the hotel was directly in the way, but for the moment the hotel faded from his thoughts and he saw only tiny, blonde Martha. She was reason enough for him to make every dollar possible. Now suddenly he couldn't quiet the feeling that he was going to have to do some things he didn't like if he expected to collect his salary.

As Reed watched, the man came out of the hotel. Stopping just outside the door, he ran his eyes up and down the street. They paused for a long moment on Reed, then skipped on down the street, taking in every store front. Finally the man went to his horse and mounted, reining back the way he had come.

The uneasiness began to drain out of Reed, then suddenly returned stronger than ever. The man went no farther than the livery stable, a block beyond the hotel. There he swung down and led his horse inside. Reed frowned. First the hotel, then the stable. That had to mean that the man was staying in town awhile.

Stepping off the porch of the marshal's office, Reed angled down and across the street to the hotel. If the man had registered, Reed could find out who he was. Not that it made any real difference. Who he was didn't matter as much as what he was. And Reed had already made up his mind about that.

The sun was beginning to warm up, but it couldn't drive out the penetrating chill that was building up in the pit of Reed's stomach. Reed's boots clumped hollowly on the hotel veranda as he crossed to the door. Moving inside, he quickly made his way to the register.

The moment Reed stepped in, he heard excited voices in the kitchen. Then Jill Larkin, who owned the hotel with her husband, Emory, came quickly through the partition doorway. Jill was not a woman to get ruffled by every stray puff of ill wind, but she was plenty ruffled now. She was well over five feet tall and, though she was nearing forty, her movements were light and quick, reminding Reed of a young panther. Right now her red hair was in disarray, and her green eyes sparkled with excitement.

"Did you see who just registered?" she demanded.

With a deft twist, Reed whirled the register around and looked at the last name scrawled there, Johnny Venango.

"Never heard of him," he said, looking up at Jill.

"I don't mean the name," Jill said. "I mean the man. He's a gunman, Reed, a killer. I've seen his kind too many times to be mistaken."

"You don't know he's a killer," Reed said slowly. "He might be a marshal on the trail of an outlaw."

"Then why didn't he go to you first?"

"Give him time," Reed said, not believing his own argument. "You know, he might be just a cowboy or a drummer who wants to look like a gunman."

"He's no cowboy," Jill said positively. "And if he's a drummer, he must be in the undertaking business."

3

"Suppose anybody in town knows him?"

"Not likely. People who live in a town such as this seldom cross trails with a man like Johnny Venango."

"He didn't tell you what he was in town for?"

Jill shook her head. "Of course not. But he has probably come to kill somebody. A man like that doesn't go anywhere for any other reason."

"Who were you talking to in the kitchen when I came in?"

"Fran Daisey," Jill said. "Couldn't you guess?"

Reed nodded. Fran Daisey's disposition demanded that she find out everything there was to know about the stranger as soon as possible.

A boot tapped lightly out on the porch, and Reed turned. Nodding to Jill, he moved toward the door. He wasn't wearing a gun. He had worn one only a few times since taking the marshal's job. There was something about Venango, however, that made a man feel undressed without a gun.

As he reached the door, he saw Tolly King, who operated the livery stable, leave the barn on a bay horse, spurring him into a gallop to the west past the schoolhouse.

Pushing through the door, Reed saw Johnny Venango sitting in one of the chairs put on the porch for those who wanted to while away some time in the shade of the veranda roof. Venango's gray, almost colorless eyes whipped down to Reed's belt, then came back to his eyes and held them as a magnet holds a nail. He made no move to get up.

In the long silence that followed, Reed had time to size up the gunman and confirm his first impression. He was tall and broad-shouldered, fairly heavy, but there wasn't an extra ounce of weight on his frame. His cheeks were hollow, accenting his

4

pale eyes and narrow, thin nose. His hair was brown and badly needed the attention of a barber, while his dusty brown hat blended with his equally dusty gray shirt and Levis. His boots were run over at the heels, and he wore no spurs. The thought flashed through Reed's mind that spurs made a noise, and a man like Johnny Venango couldn't afford to advertise his movements.

"So you're the marshal," Venango said, his voice as colorless as his appearance.

"That's my job," Reed said. "Are you staying in Rimfire long?"

Venango shrugged. "Hard to say. I never make long-range plans."

Reed looked at the gunman a moment longer, then stepped from the porch when it became obvious that Venango had given out all the information he intended to.

Moving along the street, Reed turned into the hardware store next to the hotel. Sam Upshaw was a tall thin man who had the distinction of being the town's undertaker as well as the owner of the hardware store. He seemed to take pride in trying to look the way he thought people expected an undertaker to look. He was a dark man, with black eyes and black hair just now beginning to show sprinkles of gray. He always dressed in black, as if expecting a call for his services as a mortician.

"Seen our visitor, Sam?" Reed asked.

Upshaw nodded. "Looks like a bad one. Know him?"

"He signed the hotel register as Johnny Venango. Jill thinks he is a killer. You may have some business before he leaves town."

"If he kills a certain man in town, I won't object," Upshaw said, frowning.

5

Reed started to say something, then turned and went back out into the sunshine. Sam Upshaw made no secret of his dislike for Reuben Ortega, who owned the lumber yard. But so far as Reed could determine, Ortega had given Upshaw no reason to hate him.

Reed crossed the street, where he saw Cal McBean, the druggist, peering out his big front window at Johnny Venango sitting on the hotel veranda. It wasn't often McBean showed any interest in anybody or anything around him.

"Who is he?" McBean demanded when Reed stepped through the door.

Reed read the fear in the face of the tall druggist. McBean's shaggy blond hair bushed out from his head like a worn mop, and he tugged at his long droopy moustache, which was faded almost white.

"His name is Johnny Venango," Reed said.

"What's he doing here?"

"He hasn't said," Reed replied. "He could be a saddle bum or a lawman just passing through."

"He's no ordinary saddle bum," McBean said. "You've got to find out what he wants."

"I'll find out if he wants to tell me," Reed said. "As long as he behaves, I have no quarrel with him."

"You're afraid of him, that's what," McBean said accusingly. "You've got to run him out of town!"

"He has a right to stay here if he wants to."

"You're yellow!" McBean shouted. "You're afraid to go up against him."

"Calm down, Cal," Reed said, his anger rising. "Why are you afraid of him?"

"I'm not!" McBean fairly screamed. "I just don't want his kind here."

Reed went back to the street. McBean was scared out of his wits for some reason that Reed couldn't put a finger on.

The street was almost empty now and Reed understood why when he saw Fran Daisey waddling back toward the store she and her husband ran. Fran had been doing her duty as she saw it, telling everybody about the stranger, embellishing the story where she thought it needed enlivening.

The silence of the town was almost eerie, reminding Reed of a prairie dog town immediately after an alarm has been sounded and the dogs had scurried into their burrows.

Inside his office again, Reed went to the gun rack, took down his gun belt and strapped it around his waist. He hadn't expected to wear it much in Rimfire. But then, he hadn't expected Johnny Venango to come there.

The gun felt comfortable on his hip, too much so. He had always had a special touch for the grips of a .45. Even as a youngster, he had been able to draw and fire faster and more accurately than most men. But he had never had the inner disregard for his fellow man that was so necessary in the making of a killer.

His gun speed had gotten him into bad situations twice, and he had resolved to put his gun away while he was still free to do it. He had come to Rimfire, a little town miles away from any railroad, with only two mail stages a week. It wasn't farming country, not even the best ranching country, but the few people there were peaceful, the kind who didn't fight, mainly because there just wasn't anything worth fighting over.

He had bought a small piece of land out on the creek between town and Burkley Belling's ranch. He planned to buy cattle and build a house as soon as he could get enough money. When Martha Preston came to teach school last fall, his resolve to make a home on his land become an obsession.

Jobs around Rimfire, however, were as scarce as good business opportunities. So when he was offered the marshal's star, he had taken it. In Rimfire, he hadn't expected to have to use his gun, even in the line of duty. Now he wasn't so sure about that.

The clop of horses' hoofs out in the silent street took Reed to the window. Two riders were coming down the side street between the church and Ed Daisey's house. Anyone coming into town from that direction almost had to be someone from Burkley Belling's ranch. Belling's Double B was out that way, and so was Reed's little piece of land.

Tolly King was with Belling as they rounded Daisey's house into Main Street. Reed wasn't surprised. He'd been sure Tolly had ridden out to see his uncle, Burkley Belling, when he'd left town in such a hurry soon after Venango arrived.

Tolly rode down the street toward the livery barn, but Belling turned in at the hitchrack in front of the marshal's office. He swung down, a big man, tall and broad-shouldered, his heavy muscles padded with only a little flab. He wore his perpetual frown as he thumped across the little porch and into the office.

"I came to see you about that little dab of land you own, Reed," he announced brusquely. "I need it for the new herd I'm buying. How much do you want for it?"

"It's not for sale," Reed said. "I expect to start my own little spread there some day."

"You may have to fence your land to keep my cattle out," Belling said. "I'm bringing in five hundred head."

8

Reed whistled softly. "That's a lot of cattle. They must have cost you plenty."

"That's another thing," Belling said. "The stage tomorrow will be bringing in my money to pay for those cattle. As marshal, it will be your job to see that nothing happens to it."

"Nothing ever happens to anything in Rimfire," Reed said.

"I wouldn't bet on that." Belling moved to the window and stared across at the hotel veranda. "Tolly tells me a gunman rode in this morning and settled down like he aimed to stay."

"The man didn't say anything about staying long," Reed said. "If you're worried about him, put your money in the bank when it gets here."

"I intend to," Belling said, turning back toward Reed. "But if he's after my money, that cracker-box they call a bank won't stop him."

"You're borrowing trouble," Reed said. "So far, this town has never had a more peaceful visitor."

Belling stared at Venango on the hotel veranda for a minute. "He looks like a killer to me. That's how Tolly has him pegged, too." He turned back to Reed. "How is Tolly getting along?"

Reed shrugged. "He's kept out of trouble since he took over your barn."

"Even though he's my nephew, I don't know much about him," Belling admitted. "He acts a trifle wild sometimes."

"I've seen steadier citizens," Reed agreed.

"Keep an eye on him for me," Belling said, and stamped out the door.

Reed frowned as he watched Belling mount and ride down the street past the hotel toward the livery barn. Right now he had more important things on his mind than keeping an eye on Burkley Belling's

9

nephew.

Glancing at the clock, he saw that it was almost noon. Putting on his hat, he went outside. Dinner at the hotel wasn't until twelve-thirty. He'd have time to talk to Martha at the noon hour before getting his own dinner.

Just to the north of the marshal's office was Nettie Glee's dressmaking shop. Her husband, Yancey, had the distinction of being the town drunk. However, he didn't appear drunk now as he called softly to Reed. Reed turned toward the little shop.

"What's chawing on you, Yancey?" he asked.

"Who's the stranger at the hotel?" Yancey asked nervously.

"His name is Johnny Venango. Didn't Fran Daisey tell you?"

Yancey nodded. "Sure. But I wanted it from a better source than that."

"He's not bothering anybody," Reed said.

"He will," Yancey predicted. "Sure as the sun's hot, he will."

"Maybe," Reed agreed. "But until he does, there's nothing anybody can do."

Turning down the street again, he went past the drugstore and saloon, then turned west between the bank and hotel toward the schoolhouse, a block behind the bank.

As he reached the school grounds, the door of the schoolhouse burst open, and the youngsters poured out as if a cork had been pulled from the bottom of a bucket. Two youngsters came to school from a small ranch east of town. Those two settled down now against the side of the building to eat their lunches, while the others headed for home.

"Teacher's beau has come to eat dinner with her," the little Ellis girl screamed as she ran past Reed.

Reed grinned and went on to the schoolhouse, stepping through the doorway unannounced. Seated behind the big home-made desk eating her lunch, Martha Preston looked no bigger than some of her pupils who had just left. She wouldn't weigh more than a full sack of wheat, Reed thought. He loved her hair, the color of a polished double eagle; and her eyes, bluer than the April sky outside, registered both surprise and welcome when she saw him.

"Come in, Reed. I'll share a sandwich with you."

Reed perched himself on a desk. "I'll get my dinner at the hotel."

"Anything special on your mind?" Martha asked.

"You," Reed said with a grin. "You're real special."

"Silly," she said, and took a sandwich from her lunch pail. "You don't often come here at noon. You must have a reason."

"Just thought you ought to know we've got a stranger in town. He's staying at the hotel. The whole town, including your Uncle Yancey, is as jittery as a herd of spooked longhorns."

"Is he some kind of outlaw?"

"I don't know," Reed admitted. "But he carries his gun like he knows how to use it. You might do well to steer clear of him till I find out more about him."

"I hope he's gone before Mrs. Foster's house-warming party."

"So do I. But that is just the day after tomorrow. He acts like he intends to stay awhile. I'll be up to walk you home after school."

He went back toward the hotel. As he passed between the bank and the hotel, he glanced in the side window of the bank. Owen Foster, president of the bank, was standing there staring at the hotel

11

veranda, most of which he could see from the window.

Foster saw Reed and wiggled a finger at him, then moved over toward the door without waiting to see if Reed would come in. Reluctantly, Reed turned toward the bank instead of the hotel, anger building up in him. People were acting like a flock of turkeys that had just spotted a snake.

Foster wasn't alone in the bank. The druggist, Cal McBean, and Ed Daisey, whose grocery store was right across the street from the bank, were there, too.

"You're going to have to do something about that gunman!" Daisey declared.

Reed stared at the man. He was small, with prematurely gray hair, a man with no more starch in his backbone than a blade of buffalo grass. Yet here he was demanding that Reed do something.

"As long as he behaves, there's nothing I can do," Reed said, tight-lipped.

"Now see here," McBean put in, pulling nervously on his long mustache. "We know he's a killer. There's no place in this town for a man like that."

"How do you know he's a killer?" Reed demanded.

"Everybody is saying it," Owen Foster put in. "He certainly looks like one. He may be a hold-up man, too. You've got to do something, Reed."

"Right now he isn't bothering anybody," Reed said. "Let's leave it that way."

He could see that he was wasting his breath. McBean leaned forward to get a better view of Venango on the hotel porch, but Daisey stepped back where he couldn't be seen by the gunman. Foster, a short heavy man with smoky brown eyes, stood his ground like a frightened boy, afraid to fight and afraid to run because he'd be laughed at.

"I'm going to the hotel for dinner," Reed said disgustedly.

"That gunman will eat there," Foster said quickly. "Find out what he's doing here."

Reed turned in the doorway. "If he is here to kill a man, do you think he's going to tell me all about it?"

He wheeled into the street and turned toward the hotel. Venango was still on the porch, watching. He hadn't missed a move, Reed knew. If the townspeople had paraded their fears on signs down the middle of the street, they wouldn't have exposed them in any more detail to the gunman.

As he stepped up on the hotel veranda, Reed thought he detected a touch of amusement about the thin mouth of the gunman, but he couldn't be sure. He couldn't be sure of anything about Johnny Venango.

 CHAPTER II

Owen Foster stared after the marshal as he crossed the side street to the hotel and went in to dinner. If Reed Coleman wouldn't do anything to get rid of the gunman sitting on the hotel veranda, everybody in town was in for a bad time. It could mean personal disaster for Foster if Venango was allowed to stay.

Foster moved over to the front window and looked down the street. He had sent his teller home for dinner early today. Usually Foster went to dinner first, but today he wanted to stay there until he got a chance to talk to the marshal. Well, he'd talked to the marshal, and a lot of good it had done! Now he wished the teller would hurry back so he could go home for his dinner. Aleta would be furious because he was an hour late.

The teller wasn't in sight, but Burkley Belling was, coming up the street from the livery barn. He looked as if he were heading for the bank, too. Foster frowned. Belling was a good customer in the bank, but he had been getting a little overbearing lately.

Foster moved back behind the teller's window and waited. When Belling came in, he put on a forced smile.

"Something I can do for you, Burkley?" he asked in his most pleasant voice.

"I just wanted to make sure you were prepared to take care of my money when it comes in tomorrow," Belling said. "I'm putting it in your bank until my herd gets here."

Foster wiped a hand over his half bald head. "I don't see why there should be anything to worry about."

"Then you haven't seen that gunman over at the hotel."

Foster squirmed. "I've seen him, all right. But I've got a good safe. Nothing will happen to your money."

"It better not. I'm holding you personally responsible for it." Belling spun on his heel and walked out.

Foster stared after Belling as he crossed the street to the hotel. Jill Larkin came out just then and clanged the triangle hanging from a rafter of the veranda, announcing that dinner was ready. Johnny Venango got up from his chair, stretching like a lazy cat, then went inside as though reluctant to leave his post, where he could watch the fears of the town unfold before him.

Belling slowed his pace and waited for Venango to go in before crossing the veranda and following him. Foster frowned as he watched. Burkley Belling was beginning to throw his weight around too much in Rimfire. He had been just an ordinary rancher until he had bought that herd. An additional five hundred head of cattle would make him an important man.

Foster hadn't had the slightest idea that Belling had enough money to swing a deal like that. His anger burned. Belling didn't trust the bank to handle all his money—kept most of it somewhere else and brought it in only when he needed it! He was going to be an important man now. Any man with money enough to buy five hundred cattle had to be important in a community like Rimfire. Foster didn't like it.

Foster had been the main cog in Rimfire ever since he had come here. He'd been elected mayor because he was the logical man for the job. He owned the bank and he had just built by far the biggest, most luxurious house in town. People looked up to him.

Now his world threatened to collapse around him. Belling wasn't the only threat. If it had just been Belling, Foster would have found some way to cut him down to size. But he couldn't think of anything to do about Johnny Venango.

Foster wasn't ruling out the possibility that Venango was there to rob the bank. Maybe he had heard about Belling's deal for the cattle and was there to take the money before it changed hands. Belling's money, along with the money ordinarily in the bank, would make a big haul.

As much as Foster loved money and abhorred the thought of losing any that was in his care, robbery

15

wasn't his biggest worry. Venango looked like a killer. Foster guessed that he was probably a hired killer: cold, methodical, sure. The certainty that he was the target of the gunman left a cold hard lump in the bottom of Foster's stomach.

A shadow crossed the front window, and he jumped, knocking some papers off his desk. Then he saw that it was Jill Larkin, and he let his breath escape with a whistle. He drew himself up, trying to appear calm, when Jill came in.

"This is an unusual time of day for you to come to the bank, Mrs. Larkin," he said smoothly when she stepped in the door.

"I've got an unusual boarder at the hotel," Jill said. "I thought it might be better to put what money I had on hand in your safe."

"Aren't you serving dinner at the hotel now?"

"They're eating like a herd of starving hogs. I thought while they were eating was the best time to slip away."

Foster nodded, seeing her point. She didn't trust Venango, and evidently she didn't want to antagonize him by letting him know she felt better with her money in the bank while he was around.

"What if they want something while you're gone?"

"They know everything they're going to get is right there on the table," Jill said easily.

Foster took the money. "Do you think this gunman may be a thief?"

"He's a killer, I'll wager on that," Jill said. "And I never saw a man who would kill who wouldn't steal."

"Who do you think he is after here?" Foster asked, and he couldn't keep the tremor out of his voice.

"I haven't the slightest idea. He didn't say any more than he had to this morning when he registered. And the only thing he had said at the dinner table when I left was, 'Pass the potatoes,' and 'Pass the meat.' He was eating like a famished wolf."

"Do you suppose he really is after someone here?" Foster asked hesitantly. He almost dreaded to hear her answer, yet he had to know.

"If I've got Johnny Venango tagged right, he's the kind who never goes anywhere without a reason," Jill said. "He looks like a hired gun to me. And the only reason a hired gun goes anywhere is to kill someone."

Jill took her receipt and went back outside. Foster wiped the sweat off his forehead, although it wasn't a hot day, as he watched Jill go back down the side street to the rear door of the hotel.

He wondered how much Venango knew.

That day back in Missouri was still so clear in Foster's mind that it seemed incredible that nobody in Rimfire, not even Foster's wife, suspected there was anything violent in his past. He could still picture that little town where he had been an insignificant clerk in a small store and his friend, Bud Burgess, had been the teller in the bank.

Foster had planned the robbery, and everything had gone off smoothly until he and his friend had started to leave the bank. There they'd had the misfortune to run into a deputy sheriff coming into the bank. The deputy had been killed, and Burgess had been seriously wounded. He had managed to escape with Foster, however.

A posse had been quickly formed and was soon close on their trail. Foster had seen that he couldn't escape with his friend, so he had done the only logical thing under the circumstances. He had shot his companion, who was the only one who could have positively identified him, and taken all the money.

He had tried to cover his tracks, working as a clerk in stores from Texas to Nebraska, until he was sure the hunt for the bank's money and the man who stole it had ended. Then he had gotten the money from its hiding place and come to Rimfire, where no one would ever question the high caliber of his character. He had established the bank and had become Rimfire's leading citizen.

Through the years, the fear had haunted him that he might not have inflicted a fatal wound on his companion. He hadn't stopped to make sure. If Burgess had survived, he might still be awaiting his chance to get revenge. Every new man who appeared on the streets of Rimfire had been a potential threat to Foster until he could make sure that his mission was peaceful. The coming of Johnny Venango was the culmination of that fear in Foster's mind. Venango's mission obviously was not peaceful.

Foster's teller came back, and Foster clapped his hat on his head and started for the door. Dinner wasn't over at the hotel yet, and Foster wanted to get past the hotel before Venango came back to the chair on the veranda. The fewer opportunities Venango had to see Foster and identify him, the better Foster would like it.

He hurried up the street past the hardware store and the doctor's office. Passing the little church and the parsonage beside it where Levi Wakefield lived, he stepped onto the long plank sidewalk that angled up to the big house he had built for Aleta.

The house was bigger than any two houses in

town and sat on a little rise overlooking the town like a king frowning down on his subjects. It was right in the middle of the block, and the board sidewalk leading to it was made of two-inch-thick planks rather than the thinner inch boards used in the rest of the town. Everything about the house was of better material than had been used in the construction of the other buildings in town, even the bank. Foster had seen to that.

Foster found his wife in a rage because he was an hour late for dinner. But her fury bounced off him like rain off a tin roof today. He had too many other things pressing on his mind to let her petty rage irritate him further. Then she said something that penetrated his tormented mind like the blast of a clarion.

"How do you expect me to get ready for our housewarming if I have to wait dinner an hour for you?" she railed.

"The housewarming!" Foster exclaimed. "Aleta, you're not going to invite everybody to that, are you?"

"Why not? They'll never get a chance to attend an affair like this again in this town."

"Make sure your invitations go only to people who live here," Foster insisted.

She shook her head. "I might miss somebody. I'm issuing a blanket invitation. Nobody can say we were so snobbish we didn't invite them to our housewarming."

"There's a stranger staying at the hotel," Foster said desperately. "He's a gunman, Aleta. We don't want him at the party."

Aleta stared at her husband for a minute. "Gunmen don't come to Rimfire. You told me that yourself. You promised me that this was not a wild, untamed town."

"It isn't a wild town," Foster said. "But I can't keep wild men from coming here once in a while."

"You swore that this town would never be terrorized by uncivilized savages like so many others have been. Otherwise I wouldn't have come a step."

"Nobody is terrorizing this town," Foster said, trying to make Aleta believe something he didn't believe himself. "But we don't want this man at our party. Just his appearance would ruin the whole thing."

"If this party is ruined," Aleta warned softly, "I'll leave on the next stage out of here and I'll never come back."

"Then make sure he doesn't get an invitation."

"What's to keep him from barging in uninvited? Besides, if everybody else comes to the party and he doesn't, he'll have the whole town to himself."

Foster frowned. He didn't like the idea of Venango having the run of the town. His bank was down there. Something would simply have to be done about Venango before the party.

"The party isn't until day after tomorrow," Foster said finally. "Maybe the stranger will be gone by then."

"You'd better make sure he is," Aleta warned.

"Who do you think I am?" Foster snapped. "I can't go up to a gunman like that and tell him to get out of town."

"If you want me to stay in this flea bitten town, you'll make sure that man doesn't ruin my party," she said flatly.

Foster gulped his dinner and hurried back down the street. Sometimes he was sure his life would have been happier if he hadn't been married to Aleta.

CHAPTER III

Reed Coleman stood at his office window, face pulled down in a scowl, hands jammed into his pockets, as he watched Owen Foster go past.

Foster seldom came along that side of the street. The shortest route from his big house to the bank was along the other side, across the hotel veranda and through the dust of the narrow side street to the bank. But today he was as far from the hotel veranda as he could get.

Reed could see that Foster was scared. But then everyone in town seemed to be scared. Reed directed his scowl at the gunman, back in his chair on the porch of the hotel. Since he had ridden in that morning, the smooth easy life of the town had become a jittery explosive thing. No man had a right to do that to a town.

Hearing quick nervous footsteps on the boardwalk outside, Reed pressed closer to the window in order to see along the near side of the street. Cal McBean was coming up from his drugstore, two doors down from the marshal's office.

McBean was a prime example of what was happening to the citizens of the town. He had been the picture of serenity as long as Reed had known him, withdrawn, minding his own business. But not today.

McBean passed the window and turned into the office. He stopped there, one hand nervously twisting the end of his moustache.

"What are you going to do about that killer over there?" he demanded, breathing hard as if he had been running.

Anger surged up in Reed. "Why should I do

anything? He isn't bothering anybody."

"Everybody knows he's a killer," McBean said.

"I don't," Reed said.

"Maybe you don't, but everybody else does," McBean shouted. "You've got to get rid of him before he kills somebody."

"He's causing me a lot less trouble than the citizens of this town," Reed said.

"You're not going to do anything, then?"

"I've got no reason to as long as he behaves himself."

"You are afraid of him, aren't you?" McBean accused, wild-eyed. "You don't think you can handle him."

Reed pinched his lips together.

"Maybe," he said finally. "Maybe not."

McBean wheeled, stamping out of the office and back down the boardwalk to his drugstore. Reed watched him go, his mind wrestling with the last accusation McBean had thrown at him.

He was good with a gun, good enough so that he had started to build a reputation after the few times he had been forced to use it. That was one reason he had settled in an out of-the-way place such as Rimfire, where he'd been sure he'd never have to use his gun again.

But good as he was, he knew he had no business matching guns with a man like Johnny Venango. He'd need more than just a reputation for having a fast gun to handle Venango. He'd need the speed of a fast gun, too, and he doubted if he had it.

Picking up his hat, Reed left the office and turned up the street toward the church and the banker's mansion on the hill. When Reed first put on the star, Levi Wakefield had volunteered to help keep law and order any time Reed needed him. Reed felt he was going to need him soon.

The church wasn't a big one. Rimfire didn't need a big building to accommodate those who sought the peace and inspiration of its sanctuary each Sunday morning. Just north of the church was the small house where the preacher lived. For the last year and a half that house had been occupied by the widower, Levi Wakefield. Reed went up the short dirt path to the house and knocked.

"Come in," Wakefield called from inside.

Reed opened the door and stepped in. Wakefield was sitting at the living room table, an open Bible in front of him.

Just getting my Sunday morning sermon ready," he explained. His blue eyes twinkled. "Am I being arrested for some terrible crime?"

Reed grinned. "Can't do it till I get a little more evidence. Have you noticed our visitor?"

"Saw him down on the hotel porch a while ago," Wakefield said. "Of course, Fran Daisey came by to tell me his life history."

"She would," Reed said. "You ought to put her in your pulpit some Sunday morning. She could point out everybody's faults a lot faster than you can."

"Very likely," Wakefield agreed. "I doubt, though, if you stopped by just to pass the time with idle talk."

"I didn't," Reed said, his face sobering. "I may need some help in keeping an eye on this town until Johnny Venango decides to leave. How about it?"

Wakefield nodded. "Sure, if you don't object to having a deputy without a gun."

"It could be that a man would be safer without a gun than with one," Reed said. "Anyway, I don't expect you to do any fighting; just to keep an eye on things."

After a long silence, Wakefield asked softly, "Who's he after, Reed?"

"I don't know," Reed said. "Maybe nobody. But that's no worry of yours."

"Anything that affects the people of this town is my worry," Wakefield said. "Your job is to keep law and order. My job is to look after the spiritual health of the people. A man like Venango is a threat to the spiritual atmosphere of the whole town."

"He's something of a threat to the physical well being of everybody, too. But I see your point. I don't know that working as a deputy will help your cause much."

"It's better than doing nothing," Wakefield said. "When do you want me?"

"I may not need you at all. I thought I'd go up and talk to Mrs. Foster now and see if she'd postpone her plans for that housewarming party till Venango leaves. Want to come along?"

"So that's it?" Wakefield grinned. "You want somebody to hold your hand while you face the top socialite of the city."

Reed grinned, and the two of them went up the hill to Foster's big house. Reed was impressed every time he came near the house at the ornamentation and the massiveness of the place. They found Mrs. Foster in the yard, directing a man who was preparing the ground for shrubs and trees to blend in with the huge lawn she planned to put over the slopes around the house.

"It will take two men to keep this place up after she gets it finished," Wakefield said softly.

"I'd rather be marshal," Reed said.

Mrs. Foster saw her visitors and, leaving the gardener, came over to them. "I want to get my shrubs planted before the housewarming," she said enthusiastically. "I know they don't look like much now, but people with imagination can picture what the landscape will look like when the lawn is growing and the shrubs are in bloom."

"We came up to see you about the housewarming," Reed began. "As you probably know, we have an unusual stranger in town."

Mrs. Foster nodded grimly. "My husband was telling me. He talked as if everybody were scared to death of a lone man who just came in and took a room in the hotel."

"Your husband is about right," Reed said. "Johnny Venango isn't an ordinary man. I don't know how long he will stay, but I don't think it would be advisable to have your party while he is still here."

"Ha!" Mrs. Foster glared at Reed scornfully. "I'm not going to let one man upset my plans. It's your job to see that he doesn't."

Reed sighed and glanced at Wakefield. This was about the reaction he had expected from Mrs. Foster. She had never bent an inch to meet anyone halfway before; he shouldn't expect her to now.

"Didn't Owen tell you he was a dangerous man?" Wakefield asked.

"He said a lot of things. I gathered he thought the man might even kill somebody while he was here, or maybe lead a gang in and ransack the town. But I know Owen. He gets jumpy every time a dog barks."

"Johnny Venango could very well ruin your party," Reed said in a last effort to make Mrs. Foster reconsider. "If he is still here, I doubt if many people will feel like coming to a party."

"They'll come," Mrs. Foster said confidently. "No body will want to miss this one. You do your job, and I'll guarantee the party will be a success."

25

Reed turned back down the boardwalk, Wakefield keeping pace with him. "Maybe he won't come to the party even if he is still here," he said.

"The only reason he'd go would be because it fits into his plans," Wakefield said. As they reached the parsonage door, he added, "I take it you want me to watch him if he doesn't go to the party."

"I had that in mind," Reed said. "I have a big date for that party. I'd hate to miss it. The housewarming is still two days away, though, and a lot can happen between now and then."

After leaving Wakefield at the parsonage, Reed turned across the street to the lumber yard. Reuben Ortega was alone there, restacking a pile of lumber.

"The freighters dumped the last two loads of lumber they brought in without paying, any attention to the length of the boards," Ortega explained. "So I've got to sort it all out and restack it."

"How is business?" Reed asked.

Ortega shrugged. "All right. I'm not liable to sell as much lumber as I did while Owen Foster was building his house, but everybody builds something at one time or another."

"I suppose you're planning to go to the house. warming?"

Ortega grinned. "You bet. We'll all go, even the kids. They'll find things to nibble on there that they don't get at home." His face sobered. "What are you going to do about that stranger?"

Reed frowned. "You worried about him, too?"

"Only because they say he came here to kill somebody. I don't like that."

"Who said that? Fran Daisey?"

"Well, she was the first one who said it," Ortega admitted. "He does look like a killer."

"Nobody knows what he's here for," Reed said.

"Maybe he came to run me out of town."

"Why would he do that?" Reed demanded.

"Sam Upshaw said he was going to do it. I dared him to try it, because I don't think he's man enough to do it himself. But maybe he hired this gunman to do it for him."

"Just what does Upshaw have against you?"

Ortega looked at Reed with worried eyes. "I don't know. I've never done anything to hurt him. But he hates me; says he can't live in the same town with a dirty greaser."

Reed scowled. "Nobody's making him stay here. Let him leave."

"I wouldn't worry about it if it was just me," Ortega said. "I'd fight Upshaw or anybody he brought in. But I've got a wife and three youngsters. What about them, if anything happens to me?"

"Nothing's going to happen to you," Reed promised hotly. "I figure Upshaw is mostly blow. As for the gunman, he'd hardly stoop to taking a cowardly job like running somebody out of town."

Reed went back outside, his anger simmering.

He resolved to thresh this out with Upshaw right away, but as he passed the dressmaker's shop, he saw that Burkley Belling was waiting for him. He met the rancher on the little porch of his office.

"Thought you'd gone home long ago," Reed said.

Belling shook his head. "I've been down talking to Tolly. That kid worries me, Reed. He's got some wild ideas."

Reed nodded. "I know. But he's your nephew, not mine."

"Sometimes I wish he wasn't. I'm never sure what he's going to do next."

"Isn't he running your barn all right?"

"As far as I can see, everything is fine. But he's

got some dangerous ideas about what should be done about this gunman, Venango."

"And you don't agree with him?" Reed asked, looking across the street at Venango, still lounging in the chair on the hotel veranda.

"I agree that something ought to be done, but it should be done legally. Tolly's ideas don't always stay within the law. You'll have to watch him, Reed."

"It seems I have to watch everybody," Reed said. "If you're worried that Tolly will get in trouble, why don't you take him out to the ranch where you can keep an eye on him?"

"I can't do that," Belling said. "He's the only man I've got to run my livery barn. If you get that gunman out of town, he'll be all right. Venango is the one who has upset Tolly."

"He has upset everybody," Reed said, "even you. But there's nothing I can do about it. You'd better talk to Tolly and tell him to keep his nose clean."

"He won't listen to me," Belling said. "Thinks I'm babying him, and he won't stand for that. As long as he's in town, he's your responsibility."

Reed looked down the street at the livery barn. Tolly King was standing in front of the barn, staring up at the hotel. Reed knew that Belling had a right to worry about Tolly. And Reed would have to share that worry now.

CHAPTER IV

Tolly King scarcely took his eyes off Venango sitting there on the hotel veranda as though he were ruler of all he could see. But he did notice his uncle talking to the marshal. A lot of good talking would do! It was past time for talking; had been past time since the minute Johnny Venango had ridden into town. Something had to be done, and it was beginning to look as if Tolly would have to do it.

If Venango was allowed to stay in town unmolested long enough, he'd find the advantage he was looking for, and he'd kill his man. Tolly didn't need a crystal ball to see that he would surely be that man.

He was on the point of crossing the street to go around to talk to Jill when he saw Burkley Belling leave the marshal's office and come toward the barn.

"Heading for home?" Tolly asked when Belling reached the barn.

Belling nodded. "Nothing more to do here. My horse ready?"

"Will be in a minute." Tolly went to the back and brought out Belling's horse with the Double B brand on the right shoulder. "Did you have any luck talking to the marshal?"

"Reed isn't going to do anything," Belling said heavily. "I want you to cool your heels, too."

"We can't just let that killer run loose in town," Tolly said. "The marshal is pretty blind if he can't see that."

"Well, he isn't going to run him out. He set me straight on that, all right."

"There ought to be some way to make him go after Venango," Tolly said. "If we could make Reed think that Venango had broken one of his precious laws, he'd have to go after him."

"I don't think Reed figures he can take Venango."

"I doubt if he can, but he might wing him before he cashed in. Then the rest of us could take care of Venango easy enough. You wouldn't mind seeing Reed out of the way, would you?"

"I don't like to put it so crudely," Belling said. "He did cross me up by buying that piece of land I thought nobody would touch. I figured on getting it cheap when I needed it, and I need it now, with these cattle coming in."

"I'd like to see him out of the way, too," Tolly said. "I figure we can use Venango to our advantage before we get rid of him."

"You're not going to stir up a fight between Reed and the gunman, that's sure," Belling said. "And as for getting rid of Venango, that's easier talked about than handled."

"We've got to do it some way."

"Why?" Belling demanded, staring straight at Tolly.

For a moment, Tolly met his stare; then he looked away. He didn't want to tell his uncle his real reason for wanting Venango eliminated. It just might be possible that Venango wasn't really after him; then his confession would be for nothing. If he could get rid of Venango before the gunman talked, he might never have to tell.

"I figure he's after somebody in town," Tolly said lamely. "A man can only guess who it is."

Belling swung up on his horse. "Do you think he might be after you?"

"Why should he be?" Tolly asked, looking as innocent as he could.

"I don't know," Belling said. "I figured maybe you did. The best thing you can do is cut a wide path around him.

Belling put his horse to a trot up the street past the hotel, turning the corner between Daisey's house and the church.

As soon as Belling was out of sight, Tolly surveyed the town again. Nobody was coming to the

30

barn. Now was the time to do a little snooping.

Crossing the street to the blacksmith shop, he went past it to the alley, then turned up toward the rear of the hotel. He didn't want to get any closer to Johnny Venango than he had to.

At the back of the hotel, he paused, glancing in the window. Jill Larkin was in the kitchen, starting to peel potatoes for supper. Quietly Tolly crossed the little porch and opened the kitchen door, stepping inside. Jill jumped when she saw him.

"Tolly!" she exclaimed. "You shouldn't slip up on people like that."

"I wasn't slipping up," Tolly denied. "You're just jumpy, like everybody else in town. When are you going to kick that gunman out of the hotel?"

"I'm not going to," Jill said. "He hasn't done anything but eat and sit in that chair. Can't kick him out for that."

"What do you know about him?"

"No more than you do," Jill said. She stopped peeling and stared suspiciously at Tolly. "Maybe not as much."

"I never saw him before in my life, if that's what you're thinking," Tolly said.

"You're mighty curious about a man you've never seen before."

"Ain't everybody curious?"

Tolly realized he wasn't going to find out anything here. Jill not only wasn't giving out any information; she was trying to pump him. What he knew, he wasn't about to tell Jill or anybody else.

Turning, he went back out into the alley. He was going to have to be a little more subtle about his prying. The last thing he wanted was for people to get suspicious of him.

After all, he hadn't really committed any crime.

31

In fact, he had been wearing a deputy's badge when the accident happened. He wasn't wanted anywhere by the law. But there was one man who had sworn to kill him. It was that man and the men he could hire who scared Tolly.

There was no one in the streets now. There hadn't been many people in sight since Venango had ridden in that morning. Tolly felt no concern about leaving his barn unattended for a while.

Heading up the street from the barn, Tolly went to the grocery store first. If there was any rumor in the wind, Fran Daisey would know about it. He'd have to sift through what she told him, but if there was a kernel of truth in her story, he could find it.

Ed Daisey was at the front of the store, looking out of the window. Tolly didn't need to check to see what he was watching. Fran was back in the coolest part of the store, in the old rocker where she usually sat when she wasn't out chasing stories or retelling ones she had heard. The rocker had once had arms on it, but they had been taken off, mainly, Tolly guessed, because Fran just wouldn't fit between them any more. She slopped over the edges of the rocker now like a sack of oats that had been tossed over a fence post.

"Been over to see the stranger?" Tolly asked, looking over the row of canned goods as though he had come in to buy something.

"I haven't talked to him personally," Fran said. "But I found out plenty about him. He's a killer, no doubt about it."

"Anybody can see that," Tolly said. "What's he doing here?"

Fran frowned at Tolly. He realized he should have acted surprised at what she had told him. She thrived on imparting information that was startling to her listeners.

"He's after somebody," Fran said, making the rocker creak as she pushed it back and forth. "Who knows? Maybe he's after you. You haven't been here long. You never said where you came from or what you did before you came."

It was Tolly's turn to frown. Fran was pumping him for information now instead of giving out any. Anything he told her would be spread over town within the hour.

"I came here to work for my uncle. I just dropped by now to see if you had heard the same story about Johnny Venango that I had."

The rocker stopped as Fran leaned forward, threatening to collapse the front legs of the chair. "What did you hear?"

"Maybe there's nothing to it, if you haven't heard it," Tolly said.

"What did you hear?" Fran half shouted, leaning farther forward.

Tolly almost laughed. She made him think of a hippopotamus balancing on a tree branch, ready to launch himself in an effort to fly. "I heard that he was here to challenge our marshal. They say he hates all lawmen."

"Why Reed?" Fran asked, settling back a little. "Have they clashed before?"

"I don't know," Tolly said, shrugging as if it weren't important. "Does a gunman like Venango have to have a reason for everything he does?"

"Maybe not," Fran said, chewing her lip in thought. "I'd sure hate to see Reed have to go up against him."

Tolly left the store. He hadn't learned anything about the gunman, but he had planted the seed of a story that might drive the marshal and Venango into the street in a fight from which only one would come back. Tolly couldn't lose in a fight like that. His world would be much rosier if neither man were alive.

Glancing at his watch, Tolly saw that it was almost two-thirty. That would be recess time at school. He knew Martha was aware of his feelings for her, and he thought she was responding a little, but he couldn't afford to leave Reed Coleman in the field unchallenged for any length of time.

Angling through the weedy lane between the blacksmith shop and the bank, Tolly came out on the edge of the playground. The yells of the children at play had already told him his timing was right. Luck was with him, too, for Martha was out playing with the youngsters. When she saw him at the edge of the playground, she came over.

"Do you want to be in the game?" she asked.

Tolly grinned. "I'm afraid I couldn't beat them at their own game," he said. "My kind of game will be at the housewarming party at Foster's. Are you going to be there?"

"I plan to be," she said.

"I expect to be there, too," he said. "We'll have a grand time."

Turning back toward town, he moved along at a fast clip. She hadn't even responded to his last remark. She'd been polite, but she hadn't reacted as he thought she should have. Anger built up in him, not at Martha but at Reed Coleman. He was sure Reed was the reason for Martha's cool response to him. Well, if Fran Daisey did a good job of stretching the hint he had made into a full-fledged threat, maybe he wouldn't have to worry about Reed Coleman by the time the housewarming party took place.

As Tolly passed the bank again, he saw Owen

Foster staring out the window at Venango sitting on the hotel veranda. A new thought struck him. It was only a faint glimmer of an idea, but Tolly was not one to hesitate once an idea came to him.

Turning into the front door of the bank, he moved up to the teller's window. He looked past the teller to Foster, who had turned with a start when the door opened.

"What do you know about him?" Tolly asked as Foster came around to the front of the barred partition.

"Not much," Foster said. "Have you found out anything?"

Tolly moved back toward the door, and Foster followed, out of the hearing of the teller. "I've heard rumors, that's all," he said softly. "Do you, by any chance, have a lot of money on hand here in the bank?"

Foster's face blanched, and he squirmed uncomfortably. Tolly knew he had hit a sore spot. If Foster would think for a moment, he'd know that Burkley Belling would surely have told Tolly about his money coming in on the stage tomorrow. But apparently Foster was too frightened to do much reasoning.

"I will have more than usual," he said after a moment. "What about it?"

"Well, I heard that Venango was here to rob the bank," Tolly said confidentially. "I don't figure a man like Venango would come to a little town like this to hold up the bank unless he was sure there'd be a lot of money in it."

"I thought of that," Foster admitted, and Tolly was sure Foster was going to be sick. He had never seen a man so scared. "Will he strike alone, or does he have a gang?"

35

"I don't know," Tolly said. "But if I were in your place, I wouldn't wait to find out."

"What can I do?"

"I'd get the marshal to tie a can to his tail. Or if the marshal wouldn't do anything, I'd do it myself. I'd get rid of him before he had a chance to take all the money in town."

"That's all right for you to say," Foster whimpered. "But I'm no good with a gun. And there's no other way to get rid of him."

"You might be right about that," Tolly said. "But even a man who isn't in the habit of using a gun can figure out some way to handle things if he is desperate enough."

Tolly turned toward the door, leaving Foster trembling behind him. No telling what Foster would do, or if he would do anything. But Tolly knew that a scared man was a dangerous man. And certainly there had never been a man in Rimfire who was more scared than Owen Foster was right now.

If Foster made some move against Venango, even if it was an awkward attempt to kill him, Venango would have to defend himself. Once Venango did something, then Reed would have to act. That would bring Venango and the marshal up against each other.

Tolly started past the hotel, thought better of it and angled across the intersection to the saloon. No point in parading himself in front of Venango, just in case Venango was looking for him.

At the saloon, Tolly turned north to the marshal's office. He needed to make sure that the marshal was aware of the same thing Foster was expecting. Then the marshal would be quick to blame Venango instead of Foster for anything that might happen.

"What's on your mind, Tolly?" Reed asked when

Tolly stepped in off the street.

"I've been hearing rumors that the gunman over there is here to rob the bank," he said.

"Where did you hear that?" Reed demanded.

"Several sources," Tolly lied. "Foster believes it. So does Fran."

"They're only guessing," Reed said. "Venango hasn't said anything, and nobody else has any idea what he intends to do."

"Can you think of a better reason for him being in town?" Tolly asked angrily. "You sit here and do nothing, while everybody in town loses his life's savings."

"That shouldn't worry you," Reed said hotly. "Your life's savings wouldn't fill a thimble."

Tolly wheeled out of the office. At least he was sure he had accomplished what he had gone in to do. Even though Reed denied the likelihood that Venango was there to rob the bank, he'd have to consider it a possibility now.

CHAPTER V

Reed Coleman moved to the window to watch Tolly King go down the street. Obviously Tolly wanted Reed to think that Venango was there to rob the bank. But why was it important to him that Reed think that? He was still staring out of the window when he saw Fran Daisey waddling up the street. She stopped for a minute at Cal McBean's drugstore, then came on toward the marshal's office.

"Something on your mind?" Reed asked as Fran squeezed through the door.

Fran puffed a minute to catch her breath. "I came up here," she said dramatically, "to tell you that I found out from very reliable sources that Johnny Venango hates all lawmen and is here to kill you."

"Why did he pick me out?" Reed asked calmly.

"Like I told you, he hates all lawmen."

"Why did he come to Rimfire to kill a lawman?" Reed asked, feeling no alarm over Fran's announcement. "Why not some other town? I never saw him before."

"You haven't?" Fran exclaimed, disappointed. "I supposed you had tangled with him somewhere else to make him come here looking for you."

"Who told you he was looking for me?"

"I got it straight enough," Fran said. "Doesn't that satisfy you?"

Reed shook his head, "Who did you get it from?"

Fran scowled, and Reed could almost see her mind working, trying to think of a way to dodge the question. "Tolly King told me," she said finally.

"How did Tolly find out?"

"I don't know," Fran said angrily. "He just said he knew. Do you doubt him?"

"I sure do," Reed said.

"Well, I'd watch my back if I was you," Fran said, waddling toward the door.

"I intend to," Reed said. "Why don't you find out where Tolly got that story?"

"I just may do that," Fran said as she left the office, suddenly excited again at the prospect of more prying.

As soon as Fran was gone, Reed stepped out on the porch and looked up and down the street. There wasn't much he could do about Venango until something broke. But maybe he could do something about another problem that had been growing since Reuben Ortega had come to town.

Crossing the street, Reed went into the hardware

store. Sam Upshaw was back in the semi-dark interior, idly tapping a pencil on the counter.

"Figured out a way to get rid of that gunman yet?" Upshaw asked.

"He hasn't said boo to anybody," Reed said. "Let's let well enough alone. I came in here, Sam, to ask you a question. Just what have you got against Reuben Ortega?"

"He's a Mexican," Upshaw said, his face pulling down into a scowl. "Ain't that enough?"

"No, it's not," Reed said. "He's a decent citizen. Tends to his own business. Why does it upset you having him in town?"

"You can't trust a dirty Mexican," Upshaw said. "I know."

"Have you had any trouble with Ortega?"

"Not with him," Upshaw admitted. "But I know his kind. You can't trust them an inch. They'll slip a knife between your ribs the first chance they get."

"If he hasn't bothered you, you let him alone."

"If he hasn't bothered me, it's because I've been on the lookout. The minute I relax, he'll get me."

"I'll throw you in jail if I hear of you giving him any more trouble," Reed said.

"Don't worry," Upshaw said. "I wouldn't dirty my hands on him."

Reed went back out into the glare of the street, a sharp contrast to the gloom inside the store. Reed often wondered why Upshaw kept it so dark in there unless he thought it fit the somber mood of his undertaking parlor in the back of the store.

Glancing at Venango, Reed stepped out into the dust of the street. Maybe Fran Daisey could tell him something about Upshaw's background.

Reed found Ed Daisey alone in the store, as nervous as a rabbit in a fox den.

39

"Where's Fran?" Reed asked.

"Right where she always is," Ed said. "Snooping around trying to find out every secret in town."

"I came down here hoping she had found out a few."

"That gunman has her stumped," Daisey said. "She can't find out what he's doing here, and it's about to drive her out of her mind."

"Where is she now?"

"Over pumping Jill, I think. She figures Jill ought to know something about Venango by now. If Fran was in Jill's place, she'd know everything there was to know about him, from how many extra shirts he carries with him to which side of his teeth he picks first."

"There she comes now," Reed said, pointing across the street.

Apparently Fran Daisey had gone out the back of the hotel and crossed behind the bank before turning toward the store, because she was waddling along the south side of the bank now.

"Never saw her give anybody that wide a berth before," Ed Daisey admitted. "That gunman really has her spooked."

"She's got plenty of company in this town," Reed said.

Fran came across the street and into the store, puffing as though she'd been in a race. Flopping down on a chair, she fanned herself vigorously, although the April sun was only warm enough to feel comfortable to Reed.

"What did you find out?" Daisey asked his wife.

"No more than I already knew," Fran said disgustedly. "Seems a body can't learn anything about some people."

"Did you ever happen to find out anything about

40

Sam Upshaw?" Reed asked.

"She never just happened to find out anything," Ed Daisey put in. "With her, it's a business."

Fran glared at her husband but evidently didn't consider the remark worth the effort it would take to squelch it. She looked up at Reed. "What do you want to know about him?"

"Why does Sam hate Reuben Ortega so?"

Fran tried to lean back in her chair, but Reed couldn't see that she changed positions much. The chair was smothered no matter which way she sat.

"Sam Upshaw came from the South," Fran said. "I hear that he hates anybody with skin a different color from his. It was in south Texas that he tangled with the Mexicans. Seems there was an outlaw gang of Mexicans there, and they raided the ranch where Sam and his folks worked for a big cattleman.

"They tortured some of the men to death, including Sam's father. Sam ain't ever got over it. Every time he sees a Mexican, he gets fighting mad. Leastwise, that's the way I get it."

Reed nodded. "That makes sense. But Reuben Ortega has never done anything to hurt Sam. He's got to let him alone."

"I wouldn't bet he'll do it," Fran said. "A man with a hate as deep as that is liable to do something pretty bad."

"I'll keep an eye on him," Reed said. "He seems to be afraid of Johnny Venango, too. Any idea why?"

Fran nodded, in the height of her glory now that she had a chance to give out some of the information she had so laboriously gathered.

"Everybody seems to be afraid of Venango," Fran said. "But Sam may have more reason than some others. Could be that Venango is really after him.

You know, it's going to he interesting to see just who he is after."

"Why would Sam think he's after him?" Reed asked, trying to bring Fran back to the subject.

"Yancey Glee told me that he was in the saloon one night when Sam Upshaw was there. Sam don't go to the saloon much, you know, but when he does start drinking, he's liable to get roaring, drunk. He was drunk this night, Yancey said, and he was bragging about how he had killed two Mexicans down in Texas. That's probably why he's here now. He may have come out of Texas just two hops ahead of the Rangers."

"Then he may figure that some friend of those two Mexicans he killed has hired Venango to get him," Reed concluded.

Fran's eyes were shining. "Sure. And can't you guess who he figures is the friend of those two he killed? Reuben Ortega. Reuben hasn't been here long, but long enough for him to make sure that Sam Upshaw is the man he's looking for. Now Johnny Venango rides in. Adds up, doesn't it?"

Reed frowned. It did add up, all right. But he had to take into consideration Fran's imagination and her love for embellishing every story she retold.

Going back to the street, Reed headed for his office. When he passed the drugstore, he saw Cal McBean staring through the window at the hotel veranda. McBean had been after Reed to get rid of Venango ever since the gunman rode into town. From the intent look on McBean's face now, Reed knew there was more potential danger here than in Sam Upshaw.

CHAPTER VI

Turning away from the window, McBean went to the rear of the store. Not many people knew he kept a gun and holster there.

Strapping the gun belt around his waist, he tried to make the heavy gun ride comfortably on his thigh. Instead, he felt that in a crowd, he'd stick out like a longhorn steer in a herd of milk cows. Still, he gripped the gun and tried drawing it a few times.

The gun came out of the holster easier than he had expected. For a couple of years as a young man, he had worked on a ranch down in Kansas. That had been before his father, who had been a druggist, had persuaded him to go to school and learn the trade.

McBean had never been fast with a gun, and he was much slower now than he had been. But he was sure he could still hit a target if he was close to it. The way McBean planned to deal with Venango, that could be more important than speed.

For ten minutes he practiced with his gun.

He didn't hear the door open and wasn't aware that anyone was in the store until he heard the floor creak under the weight of his visitor. He glanced up, quickly slamming the gun back into the holster. But he was too late. Fran Daisey was standing just inside the door, staring at him.

"Something I can get for you?" he asked, trying to pretend that everything was normal.

"No. I just wondered if the marshal stopped by here."

McBean shook his head. "Why should he?"

"He's worried about that stranger in town," Fran said. "He was just down at the store, and he came up this way, so I figured he might have stopped. He's going to have to do something, and it seems

43

reasonable that he'll want several good men with him when he goes after that gunman."

McBean jumped at the excuse for practicing with his gun. "Reed hasn't called on me yet, but I can see he's going to have to ask the citizens to help him. I was just finding out if I could still handle a gun."

"What did you learn?" Fran asked.

McBean sighed. "I'm pretty rusty. In an emergency, I suppose I could make a fairly good deputy. What has the marshal found out about the gunman?"

"Nothing, much," Fran said disgustedly. "Nobody has. But anybody can see he's up to no good, sitting there studying the town and everybody in it."

McBean nodded. "I just hope the marshal does something about him soon. I'm ready to help him if he wants me."

Fran went back outside, and McBean watched her waddle on up the street. Moving over to the front door, he locked it, then went out the back and across the alley to the little house where he lived. The moment he stepped in the door, his wife bobbed her head out of the kitchen.

"What are you doing home this time of day?" she demanded.

"I can't just sit over there and stare at that gunman all day, Clara," he said. "It's driving me crazy."

Clara came out of the kitchen, a little mite of a woman, never having reached her childhood goal of five feet tall and a hundred pounds. She looked even smaller when she stood close to her husband, who was more than six feet tall and weighed well over twice what she did.

"That gunman is the marshal's problem," she said soothingly. "Why should you worry about him?"

44

"I've got plenty of reason, Clara," McBean said. "I never told you much about my life before we were married, but maybe I'd better now while I've got a chance."

"All right, Cal," she said. She dropped in a chair by the table and looked up at him.

McBean didn't sit down. The way he felt inside, he didn't think he would ever be calm enough to sit down again.

"I was a druggist down in Missouri before I came out here," he began.

"You told me that," Clara said.

"But I didn't tell you why I left my home town. There was a man there that I hated like a 'coon hates a hound. He lured my wife away from me. I never told you I'd been married before, did I?"

"It doesn't matter," Clara said.

"Well, one day he came in with a prescription to fill. Instead of giving him what the doc had prescribed, I gave him some poison. The only trouble was, when he got home, two of his relatives and a neighbor had the same sickness he had, so he shared his medicine with them. They all died."

"How did you get away?" Clara asked.

"I swore that it was an accident, that I had made a mistake. I was sentenced to prison, anyway, but my former wife evidently thought I was telling the truth. She slipped me a gun while I was still in the local jail. I broke out and got away, then changed my name. I came west and finally stopped in Ogallala. You know what has happened since then."

Clara sat quietly for a moment; then she caught her breath. "You think this Johnny Venango is a lawman after you?"

McBean shook his head. "He's no lawman. But this man I hated so much had a brother who wasn't

45

fooled by my story. Before my former wife slipped me that gun, he came by the jail and swore he'd kill me the day I got out of prison. He doesn't want the law to catch me now and take me to prison. He wants me dead. I figured he would hire a killer to track me down. Johnny Venango is that killer."

"Are you sure?"

"Can you think of anyone else in this town that a man like Venango would be after? I'm the one, all right. He's just waiting for his chance. He'll make it a fair fight in the street if I'll fight. If I won't, he'll shoot me in the back. You'd be better off if you packed up and took the next stage back to Ogallala."

"There's nothing in Ogallala for me," Clara said. "This is the best life I've ever had. I'm not giving it up."

"You don't have much choice," McBean said, "unless we can get rid of Venango some way."

Clara took a deep breath. "All right. If that's what we have to do, let's do it. I'm willing to fight for what is mine."

"Now don't go off half cocked," McBean said, seeing the determination in her face. "If we make a mistake and get that gunman riled, we'll be worse off than we are now."

"Do you have any ideas?"

"I've got a dozen ideas," McBean said. "Trouble is, I'm not sure I can make any of them work."

"We might shoot him where he sits on that hotel porch," Clara said. "Anybody who is a decent shot could do that. He ain't moving much."

"Then the marshal would hang me," McBean said. "Venango hasn't broken any law, so if somebody shoots him, Reed will call it murder, and the killer will swing."

"You might poison him."

46

"I've thought of that, too," McBean said. "But just how am I going to get him to take poison? Walk over there and stuff it down his throat?"

"You gave it to that man in Missouri as a prescription," Clara said thoughtfully.

"Sure, but I had to wait until he went to the doc and got the prescription. Venango doesn't look very sick to me."

"Maybe we can kill him and put the blame on someone else. The whole town is spooked, Fran Daisey says."

"For once, Fran is right," McBean said. "You may have something there, Clara. If I can find out who is making the loudest threats against Venango, then make it look like that man killed him, we might get away with it. But I'll have to do it pretty soon. Venango won't wait forever to call me out."

"How about doing it during that party at Foster's?" Clara suggested. "Everybody will be there, and nobody'll be able to tell who did what. If Venango doesn't come to the party, it will be easy to slip out and kill him. Nobody would know about it until after the party. Reed couldn't catch the killer then."

"That sounds fine, except that the Party isn't for two more days. Venango ain't likely to wait that long."

"If we can't wait, then we'll just do it some other way," Clara said.

McBean went back into the alley and through the rear door of the drugstore. He hadn't expected that kind of reaction from Clara. She was all right; the best thing that had ever happened to him.

Going to the front door, McBean flipped the lock so anyone from the street could come in. He doubted if anyone had come to his door while he was back at his house.

Up at the north end of the street, McBean noticed some movement and saw Mrs. Ortega lead one of her children out of the doctor's office and up the street toward the lumber yard. A few minutes later, Reuben Ortega came down from the lumber yard to the drugstore.

"Mike got sick at school," Ortega explained as he came in. "Martha sent him home, and Mary took him to the doc. Doc gave her this and told her to have you fill it." He handed McBean a slip of paper.

"Sure thing," McBean said.

Quickly he read the prescription, went to the shelves and filled it. Evidently little Mike Ortega had nothing worse than a stomachache, but it gave McBean some business and did the same for Doe Singer. It suddenly occurred to McBean that there were ways of making a man sick.

After Ortega left, McBean locked the front door again and headed for the back. Going out the back door, McBean turned north. After passing the rear of the little harness shop, he turned toward the street between the harness shop and the jail. Crossing the main street, he went on back to the alley, keeping the hardware store between him and the hotel. At the alley, he turned again, walking rapidly until he came to the rear of the hotel.

He had to know just how the rear of the hotel was laid out. He had never had occasion to come back there before. He hoped he'd be lucky enough to make his survey without being detected.

Stepping up on the rickety back porch, he was shocked at the contrast between this and the front of the hotel which the public saw. Up there, the veranda was in good repair and well painted. Neither paint nor repairs had been used on this back porch since it had been built.

Crossing the little porch, stepping over pails and boxes, he reached the back door that led into the kitchen. When he opened the door, he saw that his luck was not holding up. Jill Larkin was there, working on supper.

"Come on in, Cal," Jill said. "It seems everybody is using the back door today. That gunman is as good as a lock on the front door."

"I was just curious about your new boarder," McBean said. "How long is he going to stay?"

"You can guess that as well as I can," Jill said. "In fact, you can probably do better. He doesn't say anything. All you can do is look at him and guess, and you've had more chance to look at him than I have."

McBean nodded. Quickly he made a mental note of the lay-out in the kitchen. If he could slip in there while Jill was out front, he could easily put something in the cooking kettles.

"Do you have stew for the guests every night?" he asked, jerking a thumb at the contents of the big kettle that Jill was stirring.

Jill nodded. "Almost every night. Easy way to get rid of what they don't eat at noon. Can't afford to cook fresh for every meal."

"I understand that," McBean said, his mind settling on a plan. "Well, I'd better get back. It seems that gunman is upsetting the whole town, and I thought maybe you could tell me if he was riding on tomorrow."

"I hope he does," Jill said. "But he hasn't shown any signs of leaving."

McBean left the kitchen and went across the little porch, trying to memorize how the path wound between buckets and boxes. Of course, it might be different when he came back, and if it was dark, he'd have to be mighty careful.

Calomel would be the right drug, he decided as he made his way back to his store the way he had come. A small dose of that tasteless drug made a powerful laxative. An excessive dose would be fatal. But just the right amount would make a man mighty sick and should send him to the doctor or the drugstore looking for medicine. McBean was sure he knew how much to use, according to the amount of stew he wanted to contaminate.

He'd have to work out the details and plan it carefully so he wouldn't get caught. He probably wouldn't have time to do it tonight. But if Venango was still there tomorrow night, he'd fix the stew then. When the boarders who ate at the hotel came to him, he'd give them the medicine they needed to recover quickly from the effects of the calomel. But when Venango came, he'd give him a quick-acting poison.

CHAPTER VII

Reed shut his office door, then looked up and down the street before stepping off the porch. Emory Larkin was moving toward the hotel, but he was coming from the direction of the livery barn instead of the saloon, and that seemed strange. He spent most of his time in the saloon, either playing cards or trying to work up a game.

Reuben Ortega was just going into the grocery store down the street. Apparently Mary Ortega had remembered something she needed for supper.

Sam Upshaw came out of his hardware store and locked it. But instead of going into the hotel where he usually ate supper, he went across the intersection

50

toward Daisey's store.

Reed frowned. Upshaw and Ortega in the same store at the same time could spell trouble. Striding swiftly down the street, he turned into the store himself.

Ortega was being waited on when Reed arrived, and Upshaw was standing impatiently at the counter.

"You might give decent people some service around here," Upshaw said with a scowl.

Ed Daisey was hurrying with Ortega's order as though he expected his store to explode at any moment.

"Do you need something that can't wait?" Reed asked Upshaw.

"I need some fresh air in here," Upshaw said.

Reed jerked a thumb toward the door. "There's plenty of it out there."

"You always stick up for him, don't you?" Upshaw growled, glaring from Reed to Ortega.

"I do when he isn't causing any trouble."

"I'm going to cause plenty of trouble if he opens that big mouth of his once more," Ortega snapped, making Reed realize that this was a more explosive situation than he had imagined. Ortega picked up his groceries and pushed through the door.

"I'll say what I please when I please," Upshaw growled after Ortega.

"You start trouble and I'll buy into it," Reed warned.

He spun on his heel and went outside. Upshaw stared after him, ignoring Ed Daisey, who was waiting for his order.

Upshaw was late for supper, and he was in a black mood when he arrived, but everyone ignored him. Johnny Venango ate like a starved wolf again. Reed wondered if he had eaten anything for the last

51

week. His conversation was limited once more to requests to pass food his way.

As soon as supper was over, Reed went to his room in the hotel and changed to clean clothes. Going outside, he hesitated, looking at the blacksmith shop, closed now, and thinking of the smith, Zeke Ellis. Ellis had agreed to help him watch the town, but only in an emergency. The situation now hardly qualified as an emergency. Turning the other way, Reed went up the street toward the church and parsonage.

Levi Wakefield had just finished his supper when Reed arrived. He agreed to watch the town and report to Reed later if anything unusual happened.

"I don't figure anything will," Reed said. "Nothing ever does happen here in the evening. But with that gunman here, the town isn't the same."

From Wakefield's place, he went down the length of the main street to the livery barn. Tolly hadn't come to the hotel for supper as he usually did. Reed decided he must have had supper in the little shack where he lived across the street from the barn. Knowing how Tolly hated to cook for himself, Reed wondered why he had stayed away from the hotel supper table.

"I need a team and buggy," Reed said when he found Tolly in the front of the barn.

Tolly frowned, and his face flushed. "What do you want with a buggy?" he demanded.

"I figure on taking a young lady for a ride," Reed said, "if that is any of your business."

"A fine way to watch the town!" Tolly exclaimed. "This place is ready to blow up, and the marshal don't have anything better to do than to take a girl out buggy riding."

Anger was building up rapidly in Reed. Tolly's

jealousy grated on him. If Tolly said any more, Reed was afraid he would slam a fist into his face. It would hardly do for the marshal to be fighting with the citizens he was supposed to protect.

"Do I get that team and buggy, or do I have to hitch up myself?"

Tolly glared at Reed for another minute, then spun on his heel and went back into the barn.

"I want Trix and Dixie," Reed called after him, thinking that Tolly, in the mood he was in, might bring out a team that would run away at the drop of a hat.

In a few minutes Tolly brought out a team hitched to a top buggy. Without a word, he climbed out and handed the reins to Reed. Reed got in, and Tolly exploded.

"You won't be so high and mighty when Venango gets through with you."

"What's Venango going to do?" Reed asked.

"If you don't know that Venango is out to get you, I'll just let you find it out for yourself."

"Why should he be out to get me?" Reed held a check on the reins. Tolly could know something he didn't.

"He can't rob the bank with the marshal around, can he?"

"How do you know he's going to rob the bank?"

Tolly stared angrily at Reed. "Considering you're the marshal, you're mighty dense. Half the town knows that's what he came for. They also know that you're afraid of him. That's why you haven't run him out of town."

"I've had no reason to run him out," Reed said. "When I get a reason, I'll do it."

"Robbing the bank ain't any reason. Is that it?"

"He hasn't robbed the bank," Reed said angrily,

and clucked to the team, sending the buggy up the street.

Halting the buggy in front of the dressmaking shop, Reed went to the back door, where he found Martha waiting. A minute later, he backed the team away from the hitchrack and put the horses to a trot back down the main street toward the river.

It was pretty along the river at that time of year. Reed loved the smell of the new grass and the budding cottonwood and willow trees. The sun had disappeared, and twilight was creeping along the valley when the buggy reached the stream.

"When are you going to show me your place?" Martha asked softly.

"I've just been waiting for you to ask," Reed said. "It's up this creek about three miles. It's not quite as pretty there as it is here. There aren't any trees right where I plan to build, but I figure on setting out some."

Reed pulled the team to a stop on the top of a rise overlooking the creek and the valley. It was one of his favorite spots, and he knew it was one of Martha's, too.

They had been there no more than a minute when a rifle cracked among the willows along the creek, and the bullet tore through the canvas top of the buggy only inches from Reed's head.

Martha screamed, and Reed automatically ducked and dug his gun out of its holster. But the rifleman was out of range of the revolver. Slapping the reins, Reed sent the team leaping forward. The rifle cracked again, but the bullet completely missed the buggy.

"Hang on!" Reed shouted to Martha, and slapped the reins once more.

The team hit a full gallop, and Reed swung the

horses away from the trees along the creek. If he'd been alone, he'd have jumped out of the buggy and run toward the trees and tried to catch the bushwhacker, taking his chances on getting hit. But he couldn't risk having Martha hurt.

Another bullet thudded into the buggy, down by Reed's feet, splintering the thin wood there. But that was the last shot, as the buggy bounced out of range behind the frightened team. A half-mile from the creek, Reed pulled the team to a nervous walk.

"Who could have done that?" Martha asked, one hand still clutching her hat, which had threatened to fly off her head with every bounce of the buggy.

"I don't know," Reed admitted. "Yesterday such a thing would have been unbelievable. But today anything is liable to happen."

"Could it have been that gunman?"

Reed thought for a minute. "I suppose it's possible," he said finally. "But he hasn't shown any hostility toward me."

"You were warned he was here to kill you, weren't you?"

Reed nodded. "Sure, but I didn't believe it. Maybe I was wrong. He probably saw me get the buggy and drive up to get you. That would have given him time to get his horse and ride down to the river, providing he guessed I'd go there."

"That would be a reasonable guess," Martha said. "I can't think of anyone else who might try to shoot you."

"I can't, either. Want to ride around some more?"

She shook her head. "Let's go back to town. Whoever it was might try again if we stay out here."

"That's what I was thinking," Reed said. "If I could let him get close enough—"

"You'd get killed!" Martha exclaimed.

Reed sighed. He wasn't thinking about getting killed himself. But he couldn't risk letting the killer start shooting again while he had Martha with him.

Clucking to the horses, he lifted them to a trot back toward town.

Darkness had settled over the town when Reed drove the buggy up to the barn. A single lantern hung in the doorway. Climbing down from the buggy, Reed went to the office in the front of the barn. Tolly was stretched out on a cot he kept in the office. He roused when Reed stepped in.

"About time you got in," Tolly grumbled. "I'd like to go home, but I had to stick around till you got back with that buggy."

"Well, I'm back now," Reed said, not feeling in the mood to listen to Tolly's grumbling.

Since Reed had stopped at the barn on the way into town, he had to walk Martha the rest of the way home. She didn't seem to mind.

As soon as he had left Martha at Yancey Glee's door, Reed hurried back to the hotel. Jill was at the desk, but there was no one else in sight.

"Is Venango here?" Reed asked.

"He went up to bed just a few minutes ago," Jill said. "Is what you want important enough to wake him up?"

Reed shook his head. "I was just checking to see where he was. Has he been out?"

"I guess he's been sitting on the veranda ever since supper. I've been busy washing dishes and getting things ready for breakfast. I only came out from the kitchen half an hour ago."

Reed nodded and turned back into the street. He'd have to check with someone else to make sure that Venango hadn't left the hotel. He headed toward his office, where he had left Wakefield to watch things

56

while he was gone.

The minister was in Reed's office, reading a book, when Reed went in. "Short buggy ride, wasn't it?" Wakefield said.

"We had it cut short for us," Reed explained. "Somebody shot at me with a rifle. Did you see anybody leave town?"

"No," Wakefield said, his face flushing a little. "I've been here in the office most of the time. I figured if anything went wrong, I'd hear it, so I didn't roam the streets. I couldn't do much, anyway, without a gun."

"You didn't see Venango leave, did you?"

"No. I checked when you first left. He was still on the hotel porch then. But if he slipped out of town, he did it without making any fuss."

"If he was going out to shoot somebody, he wouldn't be likely to announce it with a brass band," Reed said.

"I'm sorry I didn't watch closer," Wakefield said. "I didn't expect trouble anywhere but right here in the street, and I knew I'd hear anything that happened there."

"It's all right, Levi," Reed said. "You can go on home now. I'll take over."

After the minister left, Reed pulled off his boots and lay down on the couch. He had a room at the hotel rented by the month, but tonight he decided to stay in his office. He turned his lamp low and set it by the front window so anyone in the street could see that the marshal was in his office. But Reed himself was back in a dark corner where he couldn't be seen even from the doorway.

It was sometime during the night that Reed was jarred out of his sleep by someone calling his name. When he recognized Martha's voice, he came fully awake.

"In here," he called. "What's wrong?"

Martha ran into the office, a robe wrapped around her. "The lumber yard is on fire!" she shouted.

Reed pulled on his boots and dashed past Martha to the street. A column of smoke was spiraling up against the night sky north of Glee's dressmaking shop. As yet, there didn't seem to be much of a blaze.

Reed ran down to the hotel and grabbed the iron hammer Jill used to call people to meals at the hotel dining room. He banged the triangle with all his might. Shouts sounded through the town, and soon lights began appearing as lamps were lit. Some men ran from their houses without stopping to light lamps.

By the time Reed got back to the lumber yard, several men were already there. Some didn't have any shirts, and a couple had forgotten to put on boots. There was a pump in the yard behind Glee's house and another at one corner of the lumber yard. Buckets were brought, and men began carrying water and throwing it on the blaze, which had started in one corner of a pile of dry lumber.

Reed grabbed a bucket from beside the back door of Glee's house and ran to the pump, where a man was working the handle furiously. There weren't enough men to form a bucket brigade, so each man carried his own bucket from the pump to the fire.

Reuben Ortega was there, his shirt on but not buttoned. He was running frantically from one pump to the other, not doing much to help put out the fire but babbling wildly that everything he owned was wrapped up in that lumber yard. Then, as Reed filled his bucket, Ortega grabbed it out of his hand and ran with it to the fire.

Reed turned back to the pump in Glee's yard and relieved the man who was pumping the water. While he pumped, Reed checked the men to see who was fighting the fire. He soon decided that every able-bodied man in town was there.

Within a few minutes, it became clear that the fighters were winning the battle. The fire was being confined to one end of the stack of lumber, and everything around it was well soaked so it wouldn't burn.

"That fire didn't just happen," Cal McBean panted, setting his bucket down by the pump to catch his breath. "That gunman must have started it."

"Why would he set a fire in a lumber yard?" Reed demanded. Nevertheless, he looked around for Venango and located him standing back out of the line of men carrying water. He was still just an observer, as he had been all day.

"Maybe he wanted to see how many men the town had," McBean said. "There's no better way to do that than to start a fire."

As the flames were reduced to a heavy smoke by the blanket of water, Reuben Ortega came over to Reed. "That was Upshaw's doing," he said. "I want you to arrest him."

"Can you prove it was Upshaw?" Reed asked.

"I know it was and you know it was!" Ortega shouted. "Who else would set fire to my lumber yard ?"

"I can't arrest Sam unless you can show me some proof that he did it," Reed said.

"All right," Ortega said angrily. "I'll find some proof in the morning just as soon as it's light enough to see."

Reed left the pump as the water carriers rested, watching the smoke for any sign of a new outbreak

59

of fire. Sam Upshaw was among the fire fighters.

There seemed to be only a small amount of damage done to the lumber yard. But if Martha hadn't seen the fire and awakened Reed, the whole yard could have gone up in smoke, and maybe some of the buildings close by, such as the dressmaking shop or the church across the street from the lumber yard.

Ortega announced that he was going to stay there and make sure the blaze didn't flare up again, so the others started straggling toward home. As Upshaw left the group, Reed moved over to intercept him.

"Where were you tonight when the fire started, Sam?" he asked.

Upshaw wheeled on Reed, his eyes flashing. "I suppose you're going to say I started that fire. I wouldn't have cared if his whole yard had burned up, but you can't blame me for starting it. I wouldn't have been here helping put it out if I had, would I?"

"I'm not blaming you," Reed said. "I was just asking where you were."

"I was tending to my own business, which is more than you're doing."

Reed frowned. He had never known Upshaw to be so touchy.

CHAPTER VIII

Reed went back to his office to try to get some sleep during what was left of the night. He was still asleep when the clop of a horse's hoofs in the street brought him out of the fog of weariness. He saw that the sun was up. It had been a long time since Reed had let the sun catch him in bed.

Rubbing the sleep from his eyes, he pulled on his

boots. By now, the sound of the horse in the street had stopped, and Reed realized he had heard it last right in front of his office.

Reed stepped to the door just as Burkley Belling stamped across the little porch.

"Kind of early, don't you think?" Reed said.

"My money is coming in today," Belling said, pushing into the office. "I figured I'd better get an early start if I was going to get you to do anything."

Reed backed over to the little stove, wondering if he should put on the coffeepot or go across to the hotel later and get Jill to give him a cup of hot coffee.

"Just what do you think I should do?"

"Run that gunman out of town," Belling said sharply. "Tolly is sure he is here to rob the bank. He's probably just waiting till my money gets here."

Irritation edged Reed's reply. "When he breaks a law, I'll do something. Not until."

"After he steals my money, you'll get off your backside and howl like a wolf with his tail in a trap," Belling snapped. "What good will it do then?"

"Just don't get the idea that you can make your own laws," Reed warned.

Belling scowled at Reed, breathing hard. "Maybe he'll decide to take the money before it gets to town. You can at least ride out and meet the stage and guard it into town."

"I'm town marshal, not the sheriff," Reed said. "I've got no more authority outside of town than you have."

Belling's face reddened, and he stuttered in his fury. "Maybe you ought to go over and tell that gunman just how to go about robbing everybody blind. You're doing everything else to help him."

Reed held his own temper with an effort. "I'll try

to make sure he doesn't leave town before the stage gets in. He can't hold it up from his chair on the hotel veranda."

"He may have a gang," Belling said. "He could be just sizing up the town before calling in his men to sack it."

"If he's figuring on that, he won't upset his plans just to hold up the stage."

Belling glared at Reed another minute, his breath rasping in his throat. Then, with an oath, he spun on his heel and stamped out to his horse.

Reed went to the window and watched him ride south down the street. At the livery barn, he reined in and hammered on the closed doors. Reed guessed that Tolly King wasn't up yet. He often slept in the office, and apparently Belling thought he was there now.

After a minute, the barn door opened, and Belling went inside. A few minutes later, he came out and left town on the road on which the stage would come in later this morning. Apparently he was going to meet the stage and guard it himself. That was fine with Reed.

The town stirred cautiously as the sun climbed higher. There were only a few people on the streets. Reed guessed it would be that way until Johnny Venango left town.

He stirred up a fire and put the coffeepot on. He'd skip breakfast. Maybe he'd go over later and get something to eat. When the time came for Martha to go to school, Reed left the office. Martha had apparently been watching for him, for she came out of Yancey Glee's living quarters in the back of the dress shop as soon as he appeared.

"Going to walk me to school?" she asked.

"Figured on it," Reed said.

62

He noted the worry in her voice, even though she tried to hide it. He glanced over at the hotel. Half an hour ago Johnny Venango had come out the front door, picking his teeth, and settled in the same chair he had occupied yesterday. Reed took Martha's arm and guided her across the street toward the doctor's office.

"This is the way we usually go," Reed said, noting the alarmed look she gave him.

It was ridiculous, Reed thought, how everyone avoided going near the gunman. He had done nothing to deserve such awe.

Passing the hardware store, they stepped up on the hotel veranda and crossed it. As they passed the gunman, Reed nodded. Johnny Venango's head barely moved in response, his eyes never leaving Reed's face.

"He gives me the creeps," Martha said after they had stepped off the veranda and turned up the side street toward the schoolhouse.

"You have plenty of company," Reed said.

At the schoolhouse, he left Martha, promising to come back and walk her home after school unless the lid blew off things before then.

Reed left his office a little before dinner time and made his way across to the hotel. He was on the porch when Jill came out and clanged on the gong to announce the noon meal. Venango got up, stretched like a lazy cat and went inside. Sam Upshaw came from the hardware store next door, making sure he locked the front door, something Reed had never known him to do before. Tolly King didn't appear as he usually did. Knowing how Tolly hated to eat his own cooking, Reed wondered about his absence from the dinner table.

The meal was a quiet one. Sam Upshaw was

particularly surly.

Reed usually enjoyed his meals at the hotel, but today he was glad when he finished and could get up and go outside. There was enough tension in the air at that table to curdle the food a man ate.

Angling across the street, he slowed his pace before stepping up to the porch of his office. Someone was inside. He had caught a sound or a movement that he couldn't identify. After a moment's pause, he strode on to the door.

Stepping inside, he saw Tolly King standing back from the window, looking across at the hotel.

"He's eating dinner," Reed said.

"He just came out and sat down," Tolly corrected him. "He's like a big frog, just sitting there waiting for a fly to land close enough for him to snap him up."

"Venango getting under your hide, too?"

Tolly wheeled to face Reed. "He's getting to everybody. You know he's here to rob the bank, don't you?"

"I don't know anything of the kind," Reed said. "Nobody knows anything about him."

"I do," Tolly snapped. "Haven't you seen him watching the bank? He's in a perfect position to set up a robbery. When are you going to run him out of town?"

Reed fought down the anger that surged up. "The law can't touch him until he breaks it. Sitting there on the hotel veranda and minding his own business isn't breaking any law."

"You're scared of him," Tolly sneered. "You've got a yellow streak down your back a foot wide. He tried to kill you once, and you're scared of him."

"When did he try to kill me?"

"Last night. He came to the barn and got his horse

and rode south out of town right after you left."

"What did he say?"

"Nothing, except to give him his horse."

"How do you know he tried to kill me?" Reed demanded.

Tolly glared at Reed. "It's all over town how somebody took a shot at you last night down by the river."

Reed thought back quickly. He had checked on Tolly and Venango, but he hadn't said anything to either of them about the shooting. The only one he had told was Levi Wakefield. Of course, the preacher could have said something about it.

"Why didn't you tell me last night when I got back that Venango had taken a horse out?" Reed demanded.

"You didn't ask," Tolly snapped. "You'll let that killer stay here till he does kill somebody." He spun on his heel, stamping out of the office.

Tolly's accusation that Venango was the one who had shot at him last night stuck in Reed's mind. Reed knew that if he wanted to keep living, he'd better locate the would-be killer before he tried again.

Crossing the street, he stepped up on the hotel veranda. Johnny Venango had watched him cross the street through half closed eyes. Those eyes were still on him as Reed stopped beside his chair.

"Did you go anywhere last night?" Reed asked.

Venango tipped his head back. His eyes came open, and he stared straight at Reed. "Where would I go?"

"I'm asking you," Reed said.

"I went to bed. Is that a crime?"

"Did you take a ride down by the creek?"

"What for? Figure I'm bringing a gang into

65

town?"

Reed was becoming irritated. Venango was answering every question with one of his own. Reed was sure Venango knew everything that happened in town. But he had the feeling that the gunman might not even know about the shooting down by the river last night.

"Somebody took a couple of shots at me last night while I was taking Martha for a ride," Reed said.

"So I did it! Naturally!" The gunman's gray eyes turned a dull slate color. "Don't push me, law dog! If I decide to shoot at you, I won't miss."

Reed met Venango's stare. He was probably right. If Venango had shot at him, he wouldn't have missed.

The rumble of wheels broke the tension, and Reed turned to see the stagecoach wheeling into the main street from the south. He stepped to the front of the hotel veranda and waited. Johnny Venango didn't leave his chair.

The coach rocked up the street and came to a halt in front of the hotel. Before it had settled down in its braces, Owen Foster and his teller came out of the bank and hurried across the side street to the coach.

Burkley Belling was right behind the coach, and he dismounted and stood by the luggage boot. He was joined almost immediately by Foster and his teller.

No passengers got off, but the driver and guard climbed down, and the guard went to the boot of the coach and began lifting out luggage to get at the box in the bottom of the boot.

"I've got a paper for somebody to sign saying I delivered this," he said, setting the box on the ground.

Foster looked at Belling, and Belling jerked a thumb at the banker. With a sigh, Foster stepped forward, his eyes flicking to Venango on the porch. It seemed to Reed that Foster and Belling were issuing an open invitation to trouble. Even if Johnny Venango hadn't heard about Belling's money coming to the bank, he'd know it now.

Reed leaned against a porch post, where he could watch everything. Venango was sitting in his chair as though he didn't give the flick of an eyelash about what went on out at the coach. But Reed was sure he wasn't missing a move that was made.

CHAPTER IX

Owen Foster felt as if a great weight were being dropped on his shoulders as he signed the receipt for the money. He wished Belling had signed it. After all, it was his money. But he knew why Belling had made Foster sign it. If anything happened to it now, this little slip of paper would prove that it had been delivered to the bank. Therefore the bank must be responsible for it.

He and the teller picked up the box and started back toward the bank. It seemed to Foster that it was a mile across that little side street. He could almost feel the gunman's eyes burning into his back, and he hurried faster with each step. The teller had to trot to keep up.

Once inside the bank, Foster heard a step behind him, and his heart almost stopped. Whipping his head around, he saw that it was Burkley Belling.

"Are you sure that safe is solid?" Belling asked as Foster and his teller put the box down and Foster started to work the combination to open the safe.

"It's the safest place in town," Foster said. "But maybe your money would be more secure out at your ranch."

"I haven't got a safe," Belling said. "Anybody could walk off with it out there."

"But you'd be right there all the time," Foster said. "There's nobody at the bank during the night."

"Maybe you'd better see to it that there is somebody here," Belling said. "This money is your responsibility now."

"I'd rather not have that responsibility."

"Either you run a bank or you don't," Belling snapped.

"I'm running a bank," Foster said hastily. "But with that gunman in town, I'm a little nervous."

"You're as skittish as a caged canary in a room full of cats. You never have been robbed, have you?"

"Never had a man like Johnny Venango in town before," Foster said, glancing out the side window toward the hotel veranda.

"I'm holding you personally responsible for that money," Belling said menacingly, towering over the smaller banker.

"It will be safe," Foster said with an assurance he didn't feel at all. "How long will it be here?"

"Until my herd arrives," Belling said. "It's on the trail now. I figure it ought to be here in two or three days. Five hundred head of young cows. That will make me the biggest rancher in this end of the state."

Foster tried to open the door of the safe, but found he had made a mistake dialing. He spun the knob and began again, wishing Belling were somewhere else.

"You've had fifteen thousand dollars in your safe before, haven't you?" Belling demanded, glowering at Foster.

"Of course," Foster said. "But adding that to what I already have makes more than I've ever kept in my safe at one time."

Belling looked through the window at Venango slouching in his chair, only partly visible from the bank window. "That makes this bank a ripe plum for that gunman and his gang."

"Gang?" Foster said, fear making his voice squeak. "Has he got a gang?"

"A bank robber usually has. Of course, he may figure he's tough enough to do this job himself."

Foster concentrated on the dial and got the big door of the safe open.

"I've got to get back to the ranch," Belling said as Foster put the money box inside the safe. "If you lose that money, I'll take every penny out of your hide."

Foster turned his head to watch the big rancher walk out the door. Then he slammed the door of the safe and spun the dial. He tried the door to make sure it was locked before rising to his feet.

Crossing to the window, he stood where he had spent half his time since Johnny Venango had ridden into town yesterday morning. Turning to his teller, Foster motioned him over to the window. "I'm going over to see the marshal," he said. "Now if that gunman comes in, you don't know the combination to that safe. Understand?"

"Sure," the teller said. "I really don't know the combination, you know. You never gave it to me."

Foster twisted uncomfortably. "Don't you dare tell him I'm the only one who knows the combination."

"What makes you think he might come in?" the teller asked.

"If he sees me leave, he may think that is the time to strike."

"Maybe you shouldn't leave," the teller said nervously.

"I've got to talk some sense into that marshal."

Foster turned to the door, hurrying out into the sunlight. He passed McBean's drugstore and the harness shop and clumped onto the lisle porch of the marshal's office.

"What are you going to do about guarding the bank now?" he demanded almost before he got into the office.

Reed was watching the banker closely. "There's nothing for me to do. I watch the town, and I'll keep on watching it. Your bank is just one of the places I watch."

"But with that fifteen thousand dollars of Belling's there, I've got a fortune in the safe."

"Are you saying your safe isn't a good place for us to keep our money?"

"No, no," Foster said hastily. "I didn't say that. It's just that, with so much money there, it's a temptation to any outlaw, especially one who is as close to it as the hotel."

Reed eyed Foster speculatively. "Maybe I should get my money out of there before Venango takes everything."

Foster fought down his anger. The marshal was making fun of him.

"Don't you have any deputies?" Foster asked.

"Levi Wakefield helps me when I need him."

Foster snorted. "What good would a preacher be when shooting starts?"

"The only shooting I've heard around town lately is people shooting off their mouths," Reed said testily.

Foster scowled. The marshal wasn't going to do anything to protect his bank. He'd take action once the money was stolen, but what good would that do? Belling would kill Foster the minute he found out the money was gone.

Foster went outside and hurried back to the bank, again avoiding the hotel like the plague. There had to be something he could do.

"He never left his chair while you were gone," the teller said as Foster stepped inside.

Foster nodded. "He's waiting for something. Belling suggested he might have a gang."

"A gang could wipe out the town," the teller said, his face pasty with fear.

They were interrupted by the arrival of Emory Larkin.

"Something I can do for you?" Foster asked, coming to the window above the counter.

Larkin's eyes raced over the room. "Could I talk to you about a loan?"

"Sure," Foster said. He led Larkin into his office behind the safe. "What do you need money for?"

"Thinking about fixing up the hotel," Larkin replied.

Instead of sitting down as most visitors did, Larkin wandered around the office, finally stopping with his back to the window. Foster paid little attention to Larkin's show of nervousness. Everybody was nervous since the gunman had come.

"I think we can loan you the money," Foster said. "When will you want it?"

"Jill and I haven't decided exactly what we want to do yet," Larkin said. "Just thought I'd better make sure I could get the money before we made too many plans. We'll let you know."

Larkin left the office and went out to the street.

71

No one else except Fran Daisey came in the bank all afternoon. As closing time drew near, Foster became uneasy. Maybe Venango aimed to hit the bank just at closing time, then lose the posse in the night chase. He'd heard of that tactic. Foster could foil that by closing early.

Fifteen minutes before his usual closing time, Foster dismissed his teller for the day, then quickly shut the back door and locked it. After double-checking it, he went out the front door and locked it.

Slipping around to the south of the bank, he went down the alley and along the back of the building. From there he crossed the street to the rear of the hotel.

"My back door has been used more in the last two days than it has in a year," Jill complained when Foster appeared in the kitchen.

"I just want to know what you've learned about Johnny Venango," Foster said.

"Only what he wants to tell me," Jill said, "And that is nothing."

"Has he mentioned any names?" Foster insisted.

Jill stared at Foster. "What names?"

Foster squirmed. He had kept his past a complete secret. He wasn't going to open the door to it now. But he had to know if Venango had been sent by his old partner, Bud Burgess.

"Burgess," he said finally.

Jill shook her head. "Unless the name is meat or potatoes, he hasn't mentioned it here."

"Burgess must be a bank robber, or you wouldn't worry about him," Emory Larkin said.

Foster jumped. He hadn't seen Larkin over in the corner. His mind had been concentrating so much on Venango that he had failed to look around. Such carelessness could be a fatal mistake; he had to be more cautious.

"Venango is going to rob the bank, you know," Larkin went on when Foster kept silent. "He could use the help of a professional bank robber."

Foster didn't argue with Larkin. His throat was so tight with fear he doubted if he could have said anything. Wheeling, he hurried back through the rear door and into the alley.

An idea suddenly hit him. What if he were to take the money out of the safe and sneak it up to his house and let everybody think it was still in the bank? Wouldn't it be safer up there where he could watch it?

Since Venango hadn't struck already, he might wait until tomorrow night when everyone would be at Aleta's big party. If Foster couldn't persuade his wife to cancel that party, he'd have to do something to protect that money.

He crossed the wide expanse between the street and his house, where grass had been planted that spring. He pushed through the door and found Aleta in the kitchen, working on something for the party tomorrow night.

"The party is off," Foster said bluntly.

His wife stopped short, with a pan in her hand halfway to the oven. She stared at him, and he realized he had blundered. Nobody ordered Aleta to do anything. After all these years, he should have known that his only chance to get her to change her mind would be with flattery and an appeal to her great capacity for sacrifice.

"We have discussed that," Aleta said distinctly, and proceeded to the oven with her pan. "Nothing is going to interfere with this party. Is that clear?"

It couldn't have been clearer. There was no way now that he could get her to cancel the party. Wheeling, he went outside again. He had to have time to think—to decide what to do.

CHAPTER X

The gong on the hotel porch clanged, and Reed headed across the street for supper. Johnny Venango got up from his chair and moved to the door just ahead of Reed. Before he stepped up on the veranda, Reed saw Cal McBean dodge across the alleyway between the rear of the hardware store and the hotel.

Frowning, Reed moved on toward the hotel door. Why would McBean be going toward the back of the hotel now? It was time for him to close his store and go home for supper.

Inside, Reed found his place at the table. Emory Larkin was seated at the head of the table in his usual spot. He didn't do much work around the hotel, but he seldom was late for meals.

Jill came in, bringing a platter of bread and a huge pot of coffee which she set at the end of the table close to Larkin.

"Stew tonight," she announced as if expecting a cheer or a groan. But neither came. Jill's stew was always pretty good, even though it was made out of leftovers from dinner.

Suddenly Johnny Venango, who was facing the open kitchen door, slammed back his chair and ran around the table toward the kitchen. Reed, along with the others at the table, stared at him. No one in Rimfire had seen Venango move quickly before. Now his actions were like those of a cat that had been waiting for a mouse and had suddenly seen it.

Venango disappeared into the kitchen, and a minute later he showed up in the doorway, prodding Cal McBean ahead of him with his gun.

"What are you doing with him?" Reed demanded, getting out of his chair.

"Ask him," Venango said.

74

Reed looked at McBean, but the druggist had his lips tightly closed. Venango prodded McBean on to the table.

"What were you doing in my kitchen, Cal?" Jill asked finally.

"I came in to see you," McBean said sullenly.

"Sit down," Venango ordered, and McBean dropped into the chair in which Venango had been sitting.

The gunman turned to Jill. "Bring on the stew. Since he came to see you, the least you can do is feed him."

Jill frowned, but she obeyed. Johnny Venango with a gun in his hand looked just as dangerous as everyone had expected he would.

Jill brought the kettle of stew in and set it on the table. Reed had dropped back into his chair. He saw nothing to indicate that Venango was going to use the gun he held.

Venango motioned with the muzzle of his gun. "Fill your bowl and eat."

"I'm not hungry," McBean said.

"Eat!" Venango's gun touched McBean's back.

The druggist quickly ladled out some stew in his bowl and started eating. It was obvious that he wasn't enjoying his supper. Nobody else made a move to fill his own bowl. When McBean's bowl was empty, Venango motioned to the kettle again. Reluctantly, McBean ladled out some more. He took only a little, and Venango grabbed the ladle and filled the bowl.

Reed was sure he saw tears in McBean's eyes as he ate the stew. When the bowl was empty, Venango nodded.

"That should be enough. Now you go home, and don't let me see you around here again as long as I'm here."

McBean slammed back his chair and dashed for the front door as if he couldn't get there fast enough.

"What's wrong with that stew?" Jill demanded, coming to the table and stirring the ladle around in it.

"I don't know that anything is," Johnny Venango said softly.

"Then why did you make Cal eat so much of it?"

"I think he put something in it," Venango said. "If he thought it would be so good for us, I figured it ought to be good for him."

Larkin frowned. "Do you suppose that sneak put poison in this stew?"

"If he did, he got a big dose of it himself," Reed said.

"Get rid of it, Jill," Larkin said. "Cook us something else."

"You'll have a late supper," Jill said irritably.

She took the kettle and disappeared into the kitchen. Larkin stared after her. He didn't like late suppers, but Jill couldn't be blamed for this. He had no intention of staying around there and staring at Johnny Venango and the marshal while he waited.

He left and wandered carelessly across the street to the saloon. Reaching the saloon, he went inside. Ike Herriott was curious about Larkin's presence in the saloon at that hour, so Larkin explained what had happened. While Herriott was thinking about it, Larkin slipped out the back door.

Once in the alley, Larkin scurried across the side street to the rear of the general store. Ed and Fran Daisey had closed the store now and gone home.

Keeping to the alley, he moved past the rear of the feed store and came to the barn. Climbing over the corral fence, he made his way into the barn from the back. Tolly was in the little office at the front,

76

munching on a sandwich he had apparently made from bread and meat he'd bought at Daisey's store. "Why didn't you come up to the hotel for supper?" Larkin asked.

"I don't like the company you have there," Tolly said. His eyes brightened. "Got something on your mind ?"

"Might have," Larkin said. "Did you see the money come into the bank today?"

Tolly grinned. "I sure did. That bank is no fit place to keep that much money."

Larkin nodded. "I was thinking that myself. Wondering if we should do something about it."

"I've got it all figured," Tolly said. "Tomorrow night while the party is on, nobody will be down here to keep an eye on the town. It will be like taking candy from a blind man."

"That's what everybody is thinking," Larkin said. "You're sitting down here where you don't hear or see anything. The whole town figures that Venango has a gang that is going to rob the bank. Half of the people have already decided that the gang will strike while we're all at the party."

Tolly scowled. "If that's right, we don't want to tangle with them."

"Exactly. With everybody waiting for the robbery tomorrow night, nobody will be expecting it tonight."

"How can we pull it off tonight?" Tolly asked skeptically.

"I've got a plan," Larkin said. "We'll be safer and surer doing it tonight. Tomorrow, people are liable to be watching. Besides, if there is anything to the talk that Venango's gang will strike tomorrow night, we've got to beat them to it."

Tolly nodded. "You're right. What's the plan?"

"You know this town by now. After ten o'clock, nothing stirs. We'll hit the bank about midnight."

"That means I've got to step things up," Tolly said. "I was figuring on tomorrow night."

It was Larkin's turn to scowl. "What are you going to step up? I'm doing the brain work for this job."

"I figure we're going to be leaving when we get this money, so I'm going to take that schoolteacher with me."

Larkin gasped. "You're completely brainless!" he exploded. "In the first place, she won't go. In the second place, if you're going to be on the run, you don't want a woman along. Besides, she'll blab everything she knows the first chance she gets. You forget that idea right now. Is that clear?"

Tolly glared at Larkin for a minute. "Well, maybe I can wait. Once I get that much money, I won't have any trouble talking her into going with me."

Larkin shook his head.

"Now you listen to me," he said. "There's room for only one brain running this. That's mine. After we get the money, I'll take it out of town and hide it, then come back. We'll both be right here tomorrow so everybody can see us. Nobody will ever suspect us if we're still in town."

Tolly shook his head, his eyes sparkling with anger. "Oh, no! You're not going to slip out of town with the money I help you get. You'd keep right on going. I know your kind."

"Maybe we'd better just forget the whole thing," Larkin said disgustedly.

"Hold on," Tolly countered. "If I don't help you rob that bank, you'll do it yourself and get all the money. I'm going to get my share."

"One man would have trouble doing it alone,"

78

Larkin said. "Somebody has to stand guard. That's why I picked you to help me. But with the crazy ideas you have, we'll never get away with it."

"My ideas ain't so crazy," Tolly said. "I—"

He broke off as a rider showed up at the front door. Larkin stepped back into the shadows beside the front office.

"I'll meet you in half an hour at the saloon," he whispered. "We can talk some more there."

"Fine," Tolly agreed, and turned to his customer.

Larkin faded back into the deep shadows and went out the back door, sure that the rider, coming in from the outside, hadn't seen him.

He hurried up the back alley and went into the rear of the saloon. Ike Herriott was waiting on a customer and barely glanced up when Larkin came in. If he noticed that it had been a long time since Larkin had gone out the back door, he gave no sign of it.

In a few minutes, Larkin went outside and across the street to the hotel. Jill should have supper about ready now. After that, he'd come back to play cards. If he decided he could trust Tolly King, he'd go ahead with the plan he had for tonight.

Jill had a light supper, complaining there wasn't much to dig up after she had had to throw out the stew.

"Anybody been over to see how Cal is feeling?" she asked as they sat down to supper.

"He can take care of himself," Larkin said. "If anything bad happens to him, we'll hear about it."

It didn't take long to eat what Jill had set out. Larkin was still a little hungry when he got up to leave. He noticed that Johnny Venango had plenty on his plate yet. He had made sure he got his share as soon as the meal started. It would be a real

79

pleasure to saddle the gunman with the bank robbery.

Crossing back to the saloon, Larkin found his favorite table and settled down. He had barely gotten into his chair when Tolly King pulled up a chair opposite him.

"Now let's hear the plan," Tolly said, sliding a bottle across at Larkin.

Larkin poured himself a drink, then looked around the room. Not many people were there tonight. It had been that way ever since Johnny Venango had come to town. There was no one close enough to overhear what he and Tolly said.

"I was in the bank this afternoon," Larkin said. "I got around to the back window and put a small chip under it. I figure that will keep it from locking, and Foster won't notice it. With a screwdriver, we can open it and climb right in. The safe itself will be no big problem. A lot of that money belongs to your uncle, you know."

Tolly grinned. "Only until I can get my hands on it. He's the high and mighty one in this country. I'd like to see him brought down a peg."

Larkin was facing the main expanse of the saloon, but Tolly was facing the door. From the sudden pasty pallor that spread over Tolly's face, Larkin knew that someone who put the fear in Tolly had come in the door.

Wheeling around in his chair, Larkin saw Johnny Venango standing just inside the swinging doors. He apparently had slipped in quietly, unlike the average cowboy barging in for a drink.

"What does he want here?" Tolly whispered.

"You, maybe," Larkin said, grinning as Tolly lifted a shaking hand to run it across his forehead.

"He couldn't—" Tolly jerked his eyes away from

80

Venango and glared al Larkin. "He doesn't know me. Why don't you find out what he's after?"

"He's not after me I know that." Larkin got up and moved easily over to the door where Venango stood, looking over the room.

"Anybody in particular you're looking for?" Larkin asked. "I might be able to help you find him."

Venango shook his head. "I'm not looking for anyone."

He backed out the door and disappeared. Larkin turned back to the table where Tolly waited.

"What did he say?" Tolly demanded before Larkin got seated.

"Nothing, as usual," Larkin said. "If he was looking for someone, he either didn't see him or didn't let on that he saw him."

"Let's hit that bank tonight," Tolly said nervously. "Then we can get out of this town."

"Thought you wanted to go to that party tomorrow night."

"What about Venango and his gang?"

"If he has a gang, they're not here now. So they won't strike until tomorrow at the earliest. But let's not lay down all our cards just yet." Larkin leaned forward and lowered his voice, although no one was close enough to hear. "We'll go ahead and try the bank tonight. If we get the money and nobody sees us, we'll hide it and stay right here in town. If we leave, they'll know we did it, and Belling will run us down if he has to chase us to China."

Tolly licked his lips and nodded. "he would, all right. But if we stay in town and Venango figures out we did it, he'll kill us for that money."

"If nobody sees us in the bank, they'll never guess who did it. You might saddle our horses and

81

leave them in the barn, just in case we do have to make a run for it. You can turn every other horse out when we pick up ours."

Tolly grinned. "They sure can't catch us on foot."

"Don't do nothing except saddle our horses," Larkin warned. "If we don't have to run, we don't want anything to throw suspicion on us."

"Sure, I understand," Tolly said. "What time?"

"Let's wait till midnight," Larkin said. "By then, everybody will be asleep. If that window opens like I figure, it should be easy."

"I'll meet you at the bank at midnight," Tolly said, and slid back his chair.

Larkin stayed at his table after Tolly left. No one came by to play cards, and Larkin didn't try to stir up a game. The few customers were not in the mood for games.

The long spring twilight lingered in the street when Larkin got up and headed for the hotel. He often slept in a room by himself on nights when he was restless. He'd do that tonight, so Jill wouldn't know when he left to meet Tolly.

He was halfway up the stairs from the lobby when he saw a small woman come staggering to the head of the stairs. She hesitated there and would have fallen down the stairs if Larkin hadn't bounded up the last steps in time to catch her. Larkin recognized Clara McBean.

"What happened to you?" he demanded, seeing the bruises on her face and her flying hair.

"That killer!" she whispered. "Take me home."

She slumped in his arms. Larkin frowned. This made no sense at all. Johnny Venango might kill a man or even a woman during a fight, but why would he beat up a tiny woman like Clara McBean?

It was no problem carrying Clara McBean down

the steps and across the empty lobby. Outside, Larkin headed for the marshal's office rather than the McBean home behind the drugstore. This was something Reed should investigate.

There was a lamp already lit in the marshal's office, and Larkin kicked in the door and carried the woman inside. Reed was sitting on the edge of his bunk, and he got up to allow Larkin to put her there.

"What happened?" he demanded.

"Says Johnny Venango beat her up," Larkin said. "You figure out why."

He turned through the door.

CHAPTER XI

Reed let go Larkin without questioning him any more. Larkin was a peculiar man. Reed was sure he knew more than he told about a lot of things. But he was as particular about what he said as he was about the cards he played in a game with high stakes.

Turning his attention to Clara McBean, he looked at the dark swelling bruises on her face. Her hair was out of its combs and hanging in twisted ropes over the little pillow on the couch. Her dress was torn where it had snagged on something. Somehow that didn't seem like the kind of thing Johnny Venango would do to a woman. But then he didn't really know Venango. Nobody in Rimfire did.

He got a rag, dampened it in the washbasin and laid it on the woman's forehead. Within a minute after the cold rag hit her face, Clara McBean heaved a deep sigh and opened her eyes. Terror came into them, and Reed laid a hand on her arm.

"You're in the marshal's office, Mrs. McBean. What happened?"

She stared at him for a minute, then breathed deeply again. "That gunman beat me up."

"Why would he do that?"

"I tried to kill him," she said after a silence.

He stared at her. There were a dozen people in town who Reed had thought might try to kill Johnny Venango. But he would never have suspected Clara McBean of being one of them.

"Why would you try to kill him?"

"He tried to kill Cal," she said. "Made him eat a bowl of stew with calomel in it."

Reed hated to show his ignorance, but he had to know. "What's calomel?"

"It's a tasteless drug that is a very strong laxative."

Reed began to see the picture. "Did Cal put that in the stew to make Venango sick?"

"I don't know," Clara McBean said. "I know he is deathly afraid of that gunman, and I'm guessing he was aiming to make him sick from the stew."

"All the rest of us would have been sick, too."

"Calomel won't kill anybody," she said. "But it will make you mighty sick. That gunman couldn't do much while he was sick."

"How about Cal?"

"He'll be awful sick, if he ate as much of that stew as he said he did."

Reed nodded. "He ate it, all right. I was there when Venango caught him in the kitchen and made him eat it. But that doesn't explain the beating you got."

"I went to the hotel when I saw that gunman go inside, and I tried to kill him. I thought it was the only way I could save my husband's life. Cal thinks now that Venango will kill him for sure."

"Venango caught you?"

She nodded. "His door wasn't locked, and I tried to slip it open far enough to get a shot at him. He was behind the door and reached around and grabbed me. That's when he beat me and took my gun."

"Did he know it was a woman?"

"I don't know," she admitted. "It all happened so fast. I got out of the room as soon as I could. I saw Emory Larkin coming up the stairs. Then I was here."

"Are you able to walk?"

She nodded. "I'll go home now."

"Not till you have Doc Singer check you over," Reed said. "You may have broken something. If Venango thought you were a man trying to kill him, he could have been pretty rough."

"He was," Clara agreed.

Reed guided Clara McBean across the street in the growing dusk. The doctor's office was closed for the day, but he lived in the back of the building. Reed pounded on the back door. When Dr. Singer answered, he explained the situation.

"You might check on Cal, too, when you get through with her," he said. "He ate a lot of that stew."

"Calomel won't kill him, but he won't be working in the store tomorrow," the doctor said. "I'll give him something to bring him out of it quick, though."

Reed turned down the street. Lights were on in most homes, but the only business place open was the saloon. Reed guessed that he might need help to keep the lid on the town through the night. After what Clara McBean had done, things weren't likely to quiet down much.

He headed south toward Zeke Ellis' place. If things got out of hand, he'd need the kind of help that the blacksmith could give him. Zeke was one of the few men in town who seemed to have no fear of Johnny Venango. In fact, Reed doubted if Zeke Ellis had ever seen the man he was afraid of.

As he neared the hotel, he saw Venango back on the porch.

"I just took a woman to the doctor," Reed said, stopping in front of Venango. "She says you beat her up."

Venango looked straight at Reed. "Would you have kissed her if she'd tried to kill you?"

Reed was surprised at the gunman's reply. "I don't know what I've have done. Why did you beat her?"

"I thought it was a man trying to gun me down," Venango said. "Who is she?"

"Cal McBean's wife."

Venango nodded. "That explains things. What did that druggist put in that stew?"

"Calomel."

For the first time since he'd ridden into town, a slight grin played across the gunman's face. "I reckon he'll be busy for a while."

"What were you doing in your room when she came after you?" Reed asked.

A frown replaced the soft lines in the gunman's face. "I figure a man can go to his room when he wants to. But if you must know, I was packing things so I could get an early start tomorrow. I don't like this town."

Reed felt a weight lift off his shoulders. "So you're leaving tomorrow?"

Venango shook his head. "I was planning on it. But I won't leave now till I get good and ready. Nobody runs me out of any town."

"Nobody's trying to run you out," Reed said.

"Just trying to kill me. Same thing. I'll go when I get ready."

Reed couldn't hold back a sigh as he moved across the hotel veranda and the side street to the bank. The town wouldn't know how close it had come to getting rid of Johnny Venango without any serious trouble. But Clara McBean had spoiled it.

At the blacksmith's house, Reed knocked. He heard the youngsters inside suddenly quiet down like mice interrupted at play. Zeke came to the door, and Reed explained the situation in town. Ellis agreed to be ready to come at a moment's notice.

"If I fire a shot, that means I need help," Reed said. "I hope nothing happens to make it necessary, but I can't be sure of anything. This town is ready to explode."

Ellis nodded. "I know. I can see it from my smithy. I'll be ready."

Reed went back to the street and headed north again. At the saloon, he turned in. Yancey Glee was at the far end of the bar, and he had consumed enough spirits to loosen his tongue. He was bragging about what he'd do to Johnny Venango if the gunman should step into the saloon at that instant.

Sam Upshaw was there, too, sitting at a table not far from the bar. This surprised Reed, because Upshaw seldom patronized the saloon. Reed made his way to the bar and waited for Ike Herriott to take care of the needs of a customer.

"You needing a drink to hold you up, too?" Herriott asked.

Reed shook his head. "Just wanted some information. What is Upshaw doing here?"

"Drinking a little and talking a lot," the bartender said. "He's ranting about that Mexican claiming he started the fire last night."

"Nobody but Ortega has accused him of it," Reed said. "I asked him some questions, but I didn't say he did it."

"Nobody here has said it, either," Herriott said. "Seems to me he's denying it too much to be convincing."

Reed nodded. The bartender might be right. Maybe it was a guilty conscience that was doing the talking for Upshaw.

"Busier than you were last night, aren't you?" Reed asked.

Herriott nodded. "I guess everybody is looking for something to bolster up his courage. Tolly King was in here earlier. He's scared spitless of that gunman."

"What's Venango done to him?"

"Nothing that I know of, and Tolly ain't figuring on giving him a chance to do anything. He talked for ten minutes with Emory Larkin over there in the corner. Don't know what those two would have to talk about. Tolly is no gambler, and Emory doesn't spend time with anybody who won't throw down his money."

"Looks to me like Yancey has been hitting the bottle too much," Reed said. "I'd better send him home."

Herriott nodded. "He has the money, so I have to serve him. He's of age. But he sure has had plenty."

Reed made his way down the bar to Yancey. Yancey grinned at Reed.

"Know what I'm going to do?" he said. "I'm going to get rid of that gunman for you. You're my friend, so I'm going to do your dirty work for you. I've faced worse men than him in my day."

"You'd better go home and sleep on it," Reed said gently. "There's no hurry."

"That's where you're wrong. There is a hurry. I've got to get rid of him right away."

Reed took Yancey's arm and led him toward the back door. Yancey never came or went from the saloon by the front door.

Outside the door, Reed pointed Yancey north up the alley toward home. "I'll call on you in the morning if I need any help."

Yancey nodded. "You do that."

He went up the alley, staggering only a little in spite of the amount of whiskey that he had put away. He was just drunk enough to be a menace to himself and anybody around him.

Reed turned back to the street and went to his office. He'd better stay here again tonight, he decided, where he was close to the pulse of the town.

A horseman came slowly up the street and reined in at the marshal's office. Reed peered out the window, but there wasn't enough light in the street for him to see who his visitor was.

When he heard him thump across the board floor of the porch, however, he guessed. Only a heavy man like Burkley Belling would make a noise like that. He stepped to the door just as Belling pushed inside.

"I see you're sitting here on your back end instead of over there guarding the bank," Belling said angrily.

"I'm the marshal of the town, not just the bank," Reed said testily.

"I figured you wouldn't be doing your job," Belling said. "That's why I came in to do it for you. I'm getting a room at the hotel overlooking the bank. I'll do the guarding for you."

"That's your privilege," Reed said. "I hope you enjoy your stay in town."

89

"You coming with me to get that room?" Belling asked.

Reed stared at Belling in surprise. He hadn't expected such an invitation. "I guess I can. Don't you think you can rent a room without help?"

"Maybe not the one I want."

Reed and Belling crossed the street to the hotel. Jill was in the lobby, and she registered surprise when Belling asked for a room on the top floor on the south side.

"Those rooms get pretty hot during the day," Jill said. "Sometimes they stay hot at night, too."

"I want a room that looks out on the bank," Belling said sharply.

Jill nodded, understanding at last. She led Belling up the stairs, and Reed followed. She opened a door into a room that had a window over the street. Directly across the street was the bank.

"This will do fine," Belling said, pulling a chair over by the window. "I'll be back as soon as I take care of my horse."

Reed returned to his office. As he reached it, he saw a movement in the alley behind. He dodged back there, his gun in his hand, then stopped as he recognized Yancey Glee. Yancey had apparently slipped away from home again and was heading for the rear door of the saloon.

CHAPTER XII

Once in the light of the saloon, Yancey Glee felt a warm glow run over him. He went straight to the bar and slapped his money on the top.

"Whiskey," he said.

Ike Herriott came down the bar to him. "Thought

the marshal sent you home."

"The marshal don't run my life," Yancey said. He took the drink that Herriott shoved across the bar to him. "Looks to me like somebody ought to be nursemaiding the marshal instead of him pushing others around."

"Reed can take care of himself," Herriott said.

"He's not running that gunman out of town." Yancey downed his drink in one mouth-warming gulp. "It looks like it's going to be up to me to do that for him."

"You'd better go home and sleep this off," Herriott said.

"I'm not going to run home and hide under the bed," Yancey declared, his voice getting louder.

His heart fluttered suddenly as the batwings banged open and he wheeled to look. If that was Johnny Venango—But it was only Tolly King. Yancey breathed easier and lifted his glass. It was empty. How he needed another drink to calm him after that scare! But the one coin in his pocket wasn't enough to buy another drink.

Tolly King came up to the bar a short distance from Yancey and slapped down some money for a drink.

"You're hitting it a little heavy tonight, too, aren't you?" Herriott said, pouring the drink for Tolly.

"I know what I'm doing," Tolly said grumpily.

Yancey slid along the bar toward Tolly. "I've handled worse than that two-bit gunman," he said. "He may have the whole town scared, but not me."

"You're scared of your own shadow," Tolly grunted.

"I don't see you running him out of town," Yancey snapped back.

"I don't claim to be a gunfighter," Tolly said.

"You do."

Yancey stretched himself to his full five feet eight inches. "I was a good hand with a gun once. I still am. I'll prove it, too, if Venango stays around long enough."

"How long will that take?" Tolly sneered. "Ten years?"

"He won't be here tomorrow. I'll see to that."

"Go on home and forget it," Herriott said, frowning.

"Aw, let him talk," Tolly said. "A little hot air ain't going to hurt us."

Yancey inched closer to Tolly. "Wouldn't want to help me run him out, would you?"

"I'm not bragging about being able to run him out," Tolly said. "You're doing that."

"I could use some help," Yancey insisted.

Tolly nodded, a frown on his face. "I know how you need to be helped." He turned to Herriott. "Pour him another drink." He laid some money on the bar.

Herriott scowled, but he poured the drink and picked up Tolly's money. Yancey gulped the drink. He had learned long ago not to linger over a free drink. If an occasion came up that called for another drink, he wouldn't get in on it if he had anything left in his glass.

Ed Daisey came in and went directly to Herriott. "Give me a bottle of whiskey. Whatever kind Cal McBean drinks."

"You buying for Cal?" Herriott asked.

Daisey nodded. "Fran heard about the trouble Cal got himself into, and she had to go over and see how he was doing. She sent me to take him a bottle of his favorite whiskey. For some reason Cal thinks that will help."

"Is he sick already?" Herriott asked.

92

"I ain't sure. But if he isn't, he knows he's going to be. That gunman made him eat enough of that stew with the calomel in it to physic a horse."

Herriott set out the bottle. "Can't see where whiskey will help any," he muttered.

"If he was a man, he'd go out and kill that gunman," Yancey said, feeling his own confidence rise as the whiskey warmed his stomach.

"Why don't you do it yourself then?" Daisey said sharply, took the bottle and headed for the door.

"I just might do that," Yancey called after him, wrinkling his nose at the disappearing Ed Daisey.

"In a pig's eye you will," Tolly said, staring moodily into his glass.

Yancey drew himself up. "You think I'm scared of him, don't you?"

"I sure do," Tolly said.

"Well, I'll show you!" Yancey said, his voice a little thick. "I was once a better marshal than Reed Coleman ever was. I can still do the job, too."

He headed for the back door. He couldn't face Johnny Venango without a gun, that was sure. He hadn't worn his gun for a long time. But he'd get it out right now and strap it on. Then he'd be ready for Venango.

Reaching home, confidence oozing from him as he considered the rich rewards that would be his once he had disposed of Johnny Venango, he went inside, barely nodding to Nettie and Martha, doing some sewing by the poor light.

Going to the bedroom, he lifted a box off the trunk in the corner and worked with the latch until the lid came open. There, right on top of the clothes, knickknacks and keepsakes that were never used any more, were his gun and holster. The gun belt was even half full of shells.

He lifted the gun out of the trunk and strapped it around his waist. It struck him as funny that he had to let the belt out one notch farther than it used to be.

He took the gun from its holster and shoved some shells into the cylinder. Once he faced down Johnny Venango, the town would shower him with glory. Then he'd laugh in the faces of those who had made fun of him.

He left the bedroom and headed for the door again. Nettie stopped him with a gasp.

"Yancey! Where are you going with that gun?"

Yancey found himself immediately on the defensive. With one hand on the doorknob, he turned to face his wife.

"I've got a job to do for the town, Nettie. Don't you interfere."

"You stay away from that gunman!" Nettie said, pushing aside her sewing and getting up. "Even when you were at your best, you might have had trouble with him. You haven't used that gun for years; Venango uses his all the time."

Nettie's words hammered through the fog building up in Yancey's brain. She was right. Every word she said was absolutely right. He didn't have a chance against Johnny Venango. But he had made his brag. And he had promised himself he wouldn't crawl.

"I'll take care of myself, Nettie," he said meekly. "Don't you worry."

He slipped out the door before Nettie could reach him.

Reaching the rear of the saloon, he made his way through the back room to the bar. But there he stopped. He didn't have any more money. There were several men in the room now, more than had been there since Venango had come to town. Surely one of them would be good for just one little drink.

He turned his back to the bar and surveyed the crowd. Tolly King was still there. Emory Larkin was at his usual table in the corner, where he gambled whenever he could get anyone to play with him. He hadn't been there when Yancey had left a few minutes ago. The surge of customers into the saloon must have brought him back.

Yancey moved across the room toward Larkin. The gambler had been good for a drink a few times before. Maybe he would be again. But before he reached Larkin, Tolly King spotted the gun Yancey was wearing.

"Hey, look at the hardware Yancey is packing," he yelled.

"Who are you going to kill, Yancey?" Larkin asked, grinning. "Venango?"

Yancey wanted a drink now more than he wanted to be ridiculed for wearing a gun. But he'd strapped on that gun for a purpose.

"That's exactly what I'm wearing it for," he said. "Nobody else in this town has nerve enough to do it."

"We can all be thankful we have Yancey to protect us," Larkin said, shuffling his cards.

The others laughed, but Yancey tried to ignore them. They'd change their tunes once he had disposed of Venango. He needed a drink to help him think of a way to kill Venango without having to face him and still make it look like a fair fight.

"I'll get rid of him; you can bet on that." Yancey drew himself up to look as tall and fierce as he could.

"You'll soon get your chance," Larkin said, his voice suddenly gone soft.

Alarm swept through Yancey. "What do you

mean?"

Larkin nodded toward the batwing doors. "I just saw Venango leave the hotel porch. He's coming this way. I figure he'll be getting here in about a minute. You can show us then how you're going to handle him."

Yancey felt the strength melt out of his knees. He wasn't ready yet. He needed another drink and needed it bad. But there wasn't time. Johnny Venango would walk through that door in another minute. Somebody, probably Larkin or Tolly, would tell him that Yancey was going to gun him down. That would be the last thing Yancey would ever hear. He had to have more time to think this out.

Without appearing to rush, Yancey moved the short distance from the table where Larkin was to the back room. If he could just get in there before Venango appeared, he'd be safe, and he'd have time to think what to do.

He was barely aware of the roar of laughter that swept over the room as he disappeared. Only after a long two minutes did Yancey realize he'd been made a fool of. Nobody was coming in that door. And Yancey had been the only one in the saloon who hadn't known it.

He slipped quietly into the big room again, and nobody seemed to notice him. He saw that Tolly King was at Larkin's table now as he made his way to it.

"I figured out how I'm going to go after Venango," he announced to Larkin. "I need a drink before I start."

"I'll bet you do," Larkin said with a grin.

"Get out of here," Tolly said. "We've got things to talk about, and we don't need an old drunk hanging over us."

"I'm no drunk," Yancey insisted. "I just need one more drink to straighten out my thinking. I've got an idea. I'll get rid of Venango for you."

Larkin shoved the bottle on the table toward him. "Take it," he said. He winked at Tolly. "I reckon we can afford it."

Yancey grabbed the bottle before Tolly ruled against Larkin's generosity. But Tolly only grinned at Larkin.

The bottle was over half full. Yancey hadn't had such a prize in his hand for a long time. He headed for the back room and out into the alley. He saw Sam Upshaw coming in the front door as he went out. But nothing interested him now but this bottle. When he got home, he'd enjoy himself as he hadn't done in months.

He passed the rear of the drugstore, then suddenly stopped behind the harness shop. If Nettie saw him bring the bottle into the house, she'd take it away from him, and he wouldn't get a drop.

Leaning against the harness shop, he lifted the bottle and took a big drink. Slowly he sank down against the building and took another swallow. He could enjoy this just as much right here, and Nettie couldn't do anything about it.

Suddenly he heard footsteps coming down the alley toward him. That could mean only one thing. Johnny Venango had come into the saloon, and someone there, probably Tolly, had told him that Yancey was going to kill him. If Venango was like most gunmen Yancey had known, he'd go looking for the man who had announced he was going to kill him. Venango was coming after Yancey right now.

As carefully and quietly as he could, he dragged the gun out of the holster at his hip. Maybe this was the chance he'd been waiting for. Venango couldn't know he was right there in the alley. He'd been looking for a way to surprise the gunman. This was it.

The footsteps were much closer now, and Yancey could see the outline of the man. Gripping the gun in both hands, he squeezed the trigger, sobbing in his fright. The shot roared like a cannon, and the man stopped in mid-stride and collapsed like a poled steer.

He'd done it! And suddenly the fog that had clouded his mind was swept away. What had he done? He had killed a man! But was it Johnny Venango? What would the gunman be doing out there? The theory that Venango was trying to find Yancey to kill him seemed ridiculous in the light of his sober consideration.

Rising to his feet, he ran in a crouch to the man he had shot. The man had fallen on his side, then sagged over half on his back. The light was very thin, but Yancey could see well enough to distinguish the heavy dark features of Sam Upshaw. He'd killed Sam Upshaw!

Wheeling, he ran down the alley toward home, running faster than he had ever run before in his life.

CHAPTER XIII

At nine o'clock Reed relaxed for the first time since morning. Wakefield had just remarked that the town was very quiet. Suddenly a shot shattered the night. Wakefield rocked forward in his chair, while Reed came to his feet.

"Where was that?" Wakefield asked.

"It was close," Reed said. "Sounded like it was right behind the jail. You stay here. I'll check it out."

The minister didn't argue but remained on the

edge of his chair while Reed checked his gun and ran toward the door.

He went down the side of the office and jail, moving slower as he neared the alley. Nothing was moving in the alley when he peered around the corner. He thought he heard the door shut over at Glee's just to the north. It might be someone coming out to see what was going on or, if it was Yancey, he might be going back inside so he wouldn't get involved. That shot should have roused most of the town.

Then he saw a lump in the dim light of the alley down at the rear of the drugstore. Forgetting caution, he ran toward it. He saw it was a man, but it wasn't until he knelt beside him that he recognized Sam Upshaw.

Bending low, he discerned the undertaker's ragged breathing. "Can you hear me, Sam?" Reed asked.

Upshaw seemed to rouse a little in response to Reed's call. Reed bent lower to hear anything he might say.

"Ortega, the dirty greaser," Upshaw mumbled. "Laid for me—"

Reed bent lower. But the effort Upshaw had made to say those few words had been too much for him. Reed looked up as he heard others running toward him. A half-dozen men were coming from the direction of the saloon. A couple more were coming from the street, running down the alleyway between the drugstore and the saloon.

Reed stood up. Someone had thought to bring a lantern, and by its light, Reed picked out Ike Herriott.

"Was Sam in the saloon tonight?"

Herriott nodded. "Not two minutes ago. He came

out the back way."

"Why did he do that?"

"I don't know," Herriott said. He peered closer at the dead man. "Is that Sam?"

Reed nodded. "It looks like someone was laying for him and shot him before he knew anyone was there. He didn't even touch his gun."

"Who could have done it?" Larkin asked, rubbing his chin.

"Was Reuben Ortega in the saloon tonight?" Reed asked.

"Not tonight," Herriott said. "That Mexican wouldn't kill anyone, anyway."

"He was mighty upset over that fire in his lumber yard," Reed said.

He didn't add that Upshaw had mentioned Ortega's name with his last breath.

"Reuben is the logical one, all right," Herriott admitted slowly. "But I just can't believe he'd do it, especially without giving Sam a chance."

Reed looked at the faces in the circle of light and picked out Dr. Singer just coming up from between the drugstore and the harness shop.

"Better take a look, Doc," Reed said.

Dr. Singer dropped on one knee and felt for Upshaw's pulse. After a minute, he rose and shook his head. "And he's the only undertaker in town, too."

"Looks like you'll have to take care of things," Reed said. "Nobody else knows anything about it." He looked at the other men. "A couple of you help Doc carry Sam wherever he says. The rest of you might as well go home."

"We've got to get the man who murdered Sam," Tolly King said. "Anybody think about that gunman, Johnny Venango?"

100

"If he wanted to kill a man, he wouldn't need to shoot him in the dark like this," Herriott said.

"Who knows how he kills?" Tolly countered. "He came here to get somebody. Maybe it was Sam."

"It's my job to find the killer," Reed said sharply. "I don't want anybody going off half cocked. Maybe it was Venango. If it was, I'll take care of it. Or it may have been Ortega, no matter how much we hate to think about it. Whoever it was, I'll find him. Just keep out of it unless I ask you to help."

"I'll wager you won't go after Venango," Tolly sneered.

Reed glared at Tolly. "I will if I think he did it," he said. But he knew that he was going to have to go after Reuben Ortega. He couldn't ignore Sam Upshaw's last words.

Reed turned down the alleyway between the buildings and came out on the street. Turning north, he passed his office, told Wakefield what had happened, then went on past Glee's to the corner. There he turned west across the street and past Daisey's house. At the far corner of the block was the little house where Reuben Ortega lived with his wife, Mary, and his four children. Three of them went to school to Martha.

It had been a long time since Reed had been faced with a job he hated to do as much as the one he had to perform now. He stepped up to the door and rapped. Mary Ortega answered.

"Is Reuben here?" Reed asked.

Mary nodded. "He and the children are in bed. He wanted to get up and go see what the shooting was about, but I wouldn't let him. Do you need to see him tonight?"

"I'm afraid so," Reed said.

He stepped in at her invitation, watching her

101

closely. Was she lying to give Reuben an alibi? If she was telling the truth, then Sam Upshaw had been wrong in identifying his killer.

Mary Ortega went into the bedroom, and a minute later Reuben came out, stuffing his shirt tail into his pants. He was barefooted. Reed decided that he could have come right home and climbed into bed. He'd have had time. He hadn't been asleep, that was obvious.

"What was the shooting about?" Ortega asked.

"Sam Upshaw was killed behind the drugstore," Reed said. "I got to him just before he died. He said you had laid for him and shot him."

Ortega's eyes widened. "That's a lie! I've been home all evening. I was in bed when we heard the shot."

"That's right, Marshal," Mary Ortega put in.

"A dying man usually tells the truth," Reed said.

"How could he have seen who killed him in that dark alley?" Reuben asked.

"The killer probably thought of that," Reed said. "I'm not saying you killed him, Reuben. But everybody in town knows there was bad blood between you two. And with Sam saying it was you, I've just got to put you in jail till we clear it up."

"You can't do that," Mary screamed. "He was right here all the time!"

"I hope you can prove that," Reed said. "Get your shoes, Reuben."

Reed waited uneasily while Reuben put on his shoes.

"It must have been that gunman who did it," Ortega said as Reed went out the door with him. "I swear I was home."

"I'll see to it you get every chance to prove that," Reed promised.

"He'd better be home by morning," Mary Ortega said from the doorway. Reed didn't like the steely tone her voice had taken on.

"Don't do something you'll be sorry for, Mary," Reuben said. "I'll be all right."

Reed was surprised to find half a dozen citizens at the jail. They watched silently as Reed led his prisoner inside. He was glad that no one except himself had heard Upshaw accuse Ortega with his dying breath. Reed certainly wasn't going to tell anyone. That could lead to a lynching, even though Sam Upshaw had not been the most popular man in town.

"You know you've got the wrong man, don't you, Marshal?" Clara McBean screamed from the porch.

Reed shut the cell door behind Ortega and locked it, then turned to look at Clara, whose bruised face was purple in the light.

"I think she's right," Fran Daisey said, waddling up to the door to face Reed. "It's that gunman."

"Do you know that he came here after Sam?" Reed asked Fran.

Fran shrugged. "Nobody knows who he came after. It could have been Sam as well as anyone. You know that nobody living in this town would kill anyone."

Reed would have agreed with that a couple of days ago. But since Johnny Venango had ridden in, nobody was the same. Murder was only an impulse away from half a dozen citizens now.

"You're all grabbing at straws," Reed said. "I can't arrest Venango unless I have some evidence that he was after Sam."

"What evidence have you got against Reuben?"

"That will come out at his trial," Reed said.

"Haven't you heard that Sam thought Venango

was sent here to get him because of some trouble he'd had with Mexicans down on the border?" Fran asked.

"I've heard so many rumors in the last two days, I can't keep them straight," Reed said. "I'll talk to Venango. Now all of you go home."

Reluctantly, the townspeople moved away, Fran Daisey being the last to go. Levi Wakefield was still there, and Reed asked him to watch the jail while he went over to the hotel to talk to Johnny Venango.

At the desk, he asked Jill which room Venango had.

"Sixteen," she said. "But he's already in bed. I wouldn't bother him till morning. He might be like a startled rattler."

Reed nodded. "I know. But a man has been murdered, and I can't sit on my hands till every suspect dreams up a perfect alibi. How long ago did he go up to bed?"

"Half an hour," Jill said.

"He didn't come down again?"

Jill shook her head. "Not through the lobby. Of course, he could have gone down the back stairs to the alley. But I doubt if he did. He may be a killer, but he doesn't strike me as the kind who would kill a man in the dark."

"Who in this town does?" Reed asked.

Jill shrugged. "Nobody, I guess. Go easy when you rap on that door, Reed."

Reed nodded and went up the stairs. He didn't like this job, but it couldn't wait.

Coming to room sixteen, he rapped on the door. There wasn't a sound inside, so he rapped again. The door suddenly jerked open, and Reed found himself staring into the bore of Venango's gun.

"What are you up to at this time of night?"

Venango demanded.

"Just asking some questions," Reed said. "How long have you been in bed?"

"Maybe a half-hour, if it's any of your business."

"I'm checking out everybody," Reed said. "Sam Upshaw was killed."

"Upshaw?" Venango nodded. "That's the hardware man. I didn't take it he was very popular in town."

"Nobody here wanted to kill him."

"How about that lumber yard man? I saw Upshaw over there just before the fire started. The Mexican was the only one who accused Upshaw of setting that fire."

"Are you saying Upshaw did start that fire?"

"I ain't saying nothing. I'm just telling you what I saw."

"Why didn't you tell me before?"

"Didn't figure it was any of my business. That Mexican had a reason to kill Upshaw. I didn't. And don't wake me up again unless you've got a better reason than this."

Before Reed could make any reply, the gunman slammed the door. Reed turned back to the stairs. He doubted if Venango had killed Upshaw, but the gunman had said little to prove his innocence. He sighed as he went down the stairs. He had only two suspects, and he didn't really believe either of them was guilty.

In his office, Reed found Levi Wakefield sitting in his chair, wide awake.

"The town's quiet now," Wakefield said. "But things don't feel right."

"I know what you mean," Reed said. "I see Dr. Singer is still in his office. I want you to go over and ask him if he'll stand guard for us tonight. Ask him to watch the north end of town and report anything to you here at the jail."

"Where will you be?"

"I'll get Zeke Ellis, and we'll watch the south end of town, particularly the bank. With all that money in there, somebody may try for it. If anything goes wrong up here, fire a gun. We'll come running."

Wakefield nodded and went across the street to the doctor's office. When he returned with assurance that the doctor would keep watch, Reed headed south to rouse Zeke Ellis.

With Ellis stationed at one corner of his blacksmith shop just south of the bank, Reed took up a position on the south side of the saloon. The hotel was directly across the street from him, and the bank was at an angle across the intersection.

Reed wasn't sure what to expect. But nothing happened, and the town remained quiet. At sunup, he checked with his helpers before going to the hotel for breakfast. He had Jill fix a tray of breakfast and took it over to Reuben Ortega. He stayed at the jail while Levi Wakefield got his breakfast, then left Wakefield in charge again and began a round of inquiries. He was tired. He had only dozed beside the saloon last night. This couldn't go on for many nights. But Reed knew that it would probably go on until Johnny Venango left town.

Reed knocked at Glee's door when it was time for Martha to go to school. Martha answered, and Reed stepped inside. Yancey was sitting at the table, holding his head in both hands.

"Hangover?" Reed asked.

Yancey jumped as though Reed had stuck him with a pin. He looked up through bleary eyes and nodded.

"Last night was a bad night," Reed said.

Yancey nodded again.

"Did you hear the shooting last night?" Reed asked.

Yancey flinched and stared at the lawman. He licked his lips before he answered. "I heard it, but I didn't go out to see about it. I figured I'd just be in the way."

Martha came then, and Reed went outside with her. He started to ask her about Yancey, but Martha had other things on her mind.

"Do you suppose Mrs. Foster will postpone her party tonight because of all the trouble in town?"

"I doubt it," Reed said, shaking his head. "I tried to get her to do that a couple of days ago, but she informed me nothing was going to stand in the way of that party."

Martha smiled. "That sounds like her. You won't have to stay and watch the town, will you?"

"I probably should," Reed said. "But I've got a heavy date for that party. I can't afford to miss it."

"You are very right about that," Martha said teasingly, "because that date has had other offers of escort to the party."

"I can imagine who," Reed said grimly. "Nothing short of another murder will keep me away."

Some of the children were already coming to school when Reed left Martha at the schoolhouse. He noticed, however, that the three Ortega children were not there. He hadn't expected them.

At the hotel, Venango was in his usual chair on the porch, but he barely glanced up out of hooded eyes as Reed went past him and into the lobby. Taking the stairs three at a time, Reed went to room eleven and knocked. Burkley Belling opened the door.

"Didn't see anything last night, did you?"

"Not a thing," Belling said. "Maybe it was because they knew I was watching. My cattle won't get here for another day or two, so I'll keep on watching. I'll sleep during the day and watch all night."

"That's your business, I guess," Reed said.

CHAPTER XIV

Tolly looked up at the hotel. He'd go see what his uncle planned to do. He was sure he wouldn't be figuring on going to the party. If he wasn't, then Tolly would have to figure a way to put him out of business while they were working on the bank.

There hadn't been much business at the barn since Venango got there. Somehow word must have reached the ranches and farms that the gunman was in town, and everybody stayed away. It wasn't likely that Tolly would miss any customers if he went up to the hotel for a while.

Crossing the street to the blacksmith shop, he went down the alleyway between it and the bank. There he turned north behind the bank and across the street to the rear of the hotel. Johnny Venango was still sitting in his chair on the hotel veranda, and Tolly saw no reason to risk a confrontation with him.

He ignored Jill in the kitchen, even turned a deaf ear to her explosion about everybody using her kitchen as a highway, and went on through the dining room to the lobby and up the stairs. At room eleven, he rapped and got an immediate answer from Burkley Belling.

"How long are you going to stay cooped up here?" Tolly asked when his uncle opened the door.

"Till my cattle get here and I get the man paid," Belling said. "I don't trust that gunman down there. I figure he has a gang just waiting to jump on this town and clean it out."

"You won't need to watch the bank tonight while everybody is at Foster's party," Tolly said. "Any robbers in town will be up there, too."

"Maybe," Belling said. "If everything down here looks dead, I might look in on the party for a minute or two. But I won't be gone long enough for anybody to break into the bank. You can count on that."

"I'm betting on you, Uncle Burkley," Tolly said. "You've always come out ahead in everything you do."

"Being careful is the way to succeed," Belling said proudly. "I figure if you do well with the barn, I might promote you to a better job on the ranch soon. Might even make you a partner some day, since I don't have any son to pass things on to."

"That sounds great, Uncle Burkley," Tolly said. "The only burr under your saddle now is that gunman down there. Maybe we could work together to get rid of him."

"What do you mean by that?" Belling asked, looking squarely at Tolly.

"Well, everybody is talking about ways to get rid of him. The whole town would be grateful to us if we did it."

"I assume you mean kill him," Belling said. "I'm not a killer, Tolly. I don't mean I wouldn't kill a man who was trying to kill me. But that gunman hasn't tried that. If he does, I'll kill him. But until he does, I'm just going to make sure he doesn't steal my money." He stared out the window at the bank.

Tolly pinched his lips together. He'd said almost

too much. That partnership in the ranch looked good to him. But he didn't believe that Belling would ever make him a partner. Tolly had run afoul of his uncle too often and had felt the lash of Belling's temper.

Tolly would take his chances on getting his money right now. That looked much more certain to him. If he and Larkin were careful, they might get away with the robbery without anyone ever finding out who had done it. The postponement from last night was merely an inconvenience. Tolly might still get that partnership if Belling didn't find out who had stolen his money.

"You ought to get a little fresh air once in a while," Tolly said. "I'm going to the party tonight. You'd better come, too."

"I'll think about it," Belling said.

Tolly went back downstairs. He doubted if Belling would leave his room tonight. He'd probably sit right by that window, wide awake, all night. Tolly's fingers touched the butt of his gun. That could cost him his life if there was no other way to get him out of the picture.

Tolly looked at the big clock in the lobby of the hotel as he went toward the kitchen. It was only five minutes until the last recess at school. He had some questions to ask Martha. Now was his chance. If he waited till school was out, Reed might show up.

He went through the kitchen and out the back door, with Jill's sharp words following him. He ignored them. How he'd like to see Reed's face when he found out that Martha had thrown him over for Tolly. She'd do that the minute she found out Tolly was a rich man. Any sane girl would.

He turned west up the street from the hotel. Before he was halfway to the schoolhouse, the door burst open and the youngsters rushed out to play during the fifteen minutes between the two afternoon sessions. Tolly waved at some of them as he went through the playground toward the schoolhouse. Martha came out to supervise their play. When she saw Tolly, she angled over to him.

"Afternoon, Martha," he said. "Going to the party tonight?"

Martha nodded. "I told you the other day I plan to go."

"How about going with me?"

Martha stared at him. "I supposed you knew I'd be going with Reed," she said finally.

"You can break that date," Tolly said. "I'm going to be a rich man some day. You'll be sorry if you turn me down."

"I'm sorry, Tolly. I can't break my date with Reed."

Anger surged up in Tolly. He fought to get a grip on it.

"How about some dances tonight, anyway?" he asked.

Martha sighed. "Well, maybe. We'll see about that when we get to the party."

Tolly knew he had pushed her as far as she was going to be pushed right now. He'd better ease off.

He had his frustration at Martha's rejection under control by the time he reached the main street. He cut straight across the street to the saloon without even looking at the hotel veranda. He knew Venango was there; he could almost feel his eyes boring into his back.

Swinging to the north, he deliberately kept his eyes off the hotel as he passed the drugstore and harness shop, then turned into the marshal's office.

Levi Wakefield was with Reed, and Tolly could see Reuben Ortega in the cell behind them. He aimed his first words at Reed.

"I just heard something I think you ought to know, Reed," he said. "Johnny Venango is saying that no lawman will be alive in this town by morning."

"Who told you that?"

"I heard him say it myself," Tolly said. "I just came from the hotel."

He watched the two men closely. They might have noticed that he hadn't stopped at the hotel. But neither showed any sign that they knew he was lying.

"He's planning something," Tolly went on. "Since you're the marshal, I figured you ought to know. And you'd better do something about it if you want to be alive to see tomorrow's sun."

Reed stared at Tolly, trying to decide how much of what he was saying was the truth. He didn't trust Tolly at all. On the other hand, he couldn't take a chance that Venango might be up to something.

Before Reed could say anything, Tolly spun on his heel and went outside and back down the street toward the barn. Reed turned to Levi Wakefield.

"What do you make of that?"

"I don't like to think anybody would tell a lie," Wakefield said slowly. "But I think that's what we just heard. It doesn't make sense that Venango would sit here for almost three days and not open his mouth about anything and then suddenly tell Tolly that he's going to kill the marshal."

Reed nodded. "Seems that way to me, too."

He looked across at the gunman sitting on the hotel porch. If it hadn't been for Clara McBean, he'd have gone this morning. At least that was what he had told Reed last night. He'd made it clear that he wasn't going to let anyone run him out of town.

"You're not going to mention this to him, are you?" Wakefield asked worriedly.

Reed shook his head. "I'll let Venango make the first move, if he intends to do anything."

"Good idea," Wakefield said.

"Think I'll go see if Yancey will watch the jail awhile tonight. We both want to be at the party some of the time, anyway. I doubt if Yancey will want to stay there longer than it takes to get some of the punch."

Wakefield grinned. "Probably he won't stay for more than one drink of that, unless it is spiked."

Reed went out the front door and turned down the alley between the jail and the dress shop to the house door toward the back of the building. Yancey opened the door when he knocked.

"If you're looking for Nettie, she's up in the dress shop," Yancey said quickly. "And Martha ain't home from school yet."

"I know it," Reed said. "I was looking for you. Wondered if I could get you to watch the jail for a while tonight. If you and Levi and I take turns, none of us will miss too much of the party."

Yancey shook his head vigorously. "I ain't guarding no jail. That's your job. Anything else you want?"

Reed frowned. Yancey was almost belligerent. "I reckon not. I just thought you might help out. You always have before."

"That's when I thought I might be a marshal again some day. I know now I won't be."

Yancey backed into the house and shut the door. Puzzled, Reed turned toward the front of the building, going into the dress shop, where Nettie was sewing at one window.

"Is something bothering Yancey?" Reed asked

from the doorway.

"Nothing that hasn't been bothering him since that gunman came to town, as far as I know," Nettie said, looking up from her sewing. "What's he done now?"

"Nothing. That's just it. He's always been begging me for a chance to help out around the jail. Now I ask him to take a turn guarding the jail tonight, and he flatly refuses. Has he been drinking too much?"

"He always does that," Nettie said. "But he hasn't had a drink today. Didn't even ask for his allowance." She laid her sewing in her lap. "Now that is strange, come to think of it. But one thing is sure. He's not drunk now."

Reed stepped out the door and started down the street, puzzled. Something was wrong with Yancey, but he couldn't imagine what it was. Maybe his fear of Johnny Venango had snapped something in his brain.

Glancing at his watch, Reed saw that it would soon be time to go to the schoolhouse to walk Martha home. She wouldn't be staying to work at the schoolhouse as long as usual after school today. Tonight was the big party at Foster's, and she seemed to think she needed a lot of time to get ready. He grinned. He wouldn't need so much preparation time, but he was looking forward to it.

After stopping at the office, Reed headed for the schoolhouse. The youngsters were gone by the time he got there. He found Martha ready to go home and eager to get outside and close the door.

"Something go wrong today?" he asked.

Martha shrugged. "Nothing worth mentioning."

"You are still planning to go to the party with me, aren't you?"

"Of course. I wouldn't go with anyone else. Not that I haven't had offers."

He grinned. "Any girl as pretty as you are will have plenty of offers. Just so you turn them all down."

"I had one today that was hard to turn down, because he just wasn't going to take no for an answer."

"Tolly?" Reed asked sharply.

Martha nodded. "Now don't you stir up any trouble over it. I think I finally convinced him I was going with you. But I thought you had a right to know."

"I'm glad you told me," Reed said. "I've warned him to stay away from you. He seems to think you'd team right up with him if I was out of the way."

"I am almost afraid of him," Martha admitted. "He seems so possessive—just as if he could buy me like a sack of sugar."

Reed decided that the next time he saw Tolly alone, he'd have it out with him.

"No trouble now," Martha said as if reading his thoughts.

"No trouble," Reed promised. "But if he bothers you again, I want to know about it immediately. Agreed?"

Martha nodded. "I think he'll let me alone now."

Reed escorted Martha to the door at the back of Glee's dress shop, then turned back toward his office. He saw Owen Foster hurrying along the street toward home.

He might not have taken a second glance at Foster if he hadn't noticed the way he was shielding something from the hotel. Since Foster had crossed the street to avoid the hotel, he was coming along right in front of the marshal's office. Reed was going to get a closer look at whatever Foster was carrying.

He stopped on the porch of the office to watch Foster. The banker's eyes were flitting to Johnny Venango on the porch of the hotel, and he didn't see Reed until he almost bumped into him.

"Something special under your coat?" Reed asked.

Foster gasped. "Just a sack of groceries that Aleta asked me to bring from the store."

Reed looked closer at the edge of the sack protruding from under the banker's coat. It looked like canvas. If it was, then it had come from the bank, not the grocery store.

Foster caught his eyes and glanced down at the bag. "I've got a lot of paper work from the bank to do, too. Aleta told me to get home early tonight, so I brought the papers home with me."

Reed nodded. He didn't believe a word of what Foster was telling him, but it was none of his business what Foster was taking home from the bank. He stepped back into the doorway of the office.

"Looking forward to the party," he said.

Foster merely grunted and hurried on up the street. Reed had a good idea what Foster had in his sack.

His suspicions were confirmed in his own mind when he saw Foster make two more trips to the bank, coming back along the east side of the street to avoid the hotel. Each time he had heavy bulges under his coat. Reed guessed that all the paper money and perhaps some of the gold had been moved out of the bank's safe to Foster's private safe in his big new house.

Reed went to the door and looked up the street to see if Levi Wakefield was coming back from his supper. Instead of Wakefield, he saw Mary Ortega. The sun was setting, and most of the people in town were getting ready for Foster's housewarming. Reed would go over to the hotel and change his clothes just as soon as Wakefield got back to keep an eye on the jail.

Mrs. Ortega came across the street from Daisey's and stepped into Reed's office. Before Reed could even greet her, she pulled a small gun from the folds of her apron, where she had kept it concealed, and pointed it at him.

"Turn my Reuben out, Marshal," she said. "He didn't kill nobody, and he's not going to hang for it."

"Now take it easy, Mrs. Ortega," Reed said cautiously, watching the woman's eyes, trying to decide how desperate she was. "Reuben is just being held until he can have a fair trial. He's not likely to hang."

"No white jury will let him off, even if he is innocent. The only way he'll get out is for me to take him out. So open the jail."

Reed could see that she meant every word. She was sure that her husband would hang unless she broke him out of jail. He believed that she would shoot him if necessary to free Reuben.

"I told you that he'll get a fair trial. I'll see to that."

"You can't make a jury turn Reuben loose." She moved closer, her gun still pointed directly at Reed. "It won't be no worse for me or the kids if I have to kill a marshal to get him free."

Reed saw that she had thought it out carefully. Nothing he could say was going to change her mind. But he had never had a prisoner taken from him, and he didn't like the idea now.

He was debating whether to yield to Mary Ortega's demands or try some trick to get the gun away from her when he saw Yancey Glee come into the office, directly behind Mrs. Ortega. Either she wasn't aware that someone had come in, or she was determined not to be diverted from the business at hand, for she didn't take her eyes off Reed.

"Shooting a marshal is a pretty serious business," Reed said, his eyes slipping past Mrs. Ortega to Yancey.

Yancey stared at Mrs. Ortega, then moved forward very softly. With a sudden sweep of his arms, he pinned both her arms to her side, knocking the gun down toward the floor. Her grip loosened, and the gun clattered at her feet.

Reed scooped up the gun, and Yancey released Mrs. Ortega. With a wild sob, she wheeled and ran from the office. Reed let her go, although what she had done should have put her in the jail cell with her husband.

"Thanks, Yancey," Reed said. "Have you changed your mind about guarding the jail tonight?"

Yancey shook his head, his face haggard. He moved over to the chair by the desk and slumped in it.

"I saw Mary come in," Yancey said, "and I guessed what she was up to. I knew then I had to do something. I know that Reuben didn't kill Sam Upshaw."

"You do?" Reed moved closer to Yancey. "Who did?"

"I did," Yancey said miserably. "I was drunk. I was trying to shape up to face Venango. When I heard someone coming down the alley, I thought it was Venango coming to get me. I shot before I saw who it was." He looked up at Reed through

118

bloodshot eyes. "When will they hang me?"

Reed was having trouble collecting his wits after the shock of what Yancey had told him. "You'll get a trial," he said. "You won't hang, I'm sure. It was an accident."

"The only accident was that it happened to be Sam Upshaw instead of Johnny Venango," Yancey said.

Reed nodded. "A jury will have to decide. But they only hang for first degree murder, and you didn't deliberately set out to kill Sam Upshaw."

He got the key from the hook and unlocked the door. Reuben Ortega came out, looking sympathetically toward Yancey. He had heard everything and didn't even need to be told he was free. He disappeared out the door, while Yancey got up slowly and went into the cell.

Levi Wakefield came in from his supper, and Reed told him why he had a different prisoner to guard.

"Nobody will bother you, I'm sure," he said. "Yancey is far better liked in this town than Sam Upshaw was. And most people will understand what happened. I'll have to tell Nettie. Then I'll get ready and take Martha to the party, if she still wants to go under the circumstances. I'll come back down later and let you get in on some of the party."

"Don't break up your evening," Wakefield said. "That isn't exactly the kind of party a preacher ought to go to, anyway. You can come back when the party is over and sleep here. I'll go home then."

"Thanks, Levi. I appreciate this."

Reed went outside, going first to Glee's to tell Nettie what Yancey had admitted doing. Martha was horrified as Reed explained, but Nettie's expression barely changed.

119

"I'm not too surprised," she said in despair. "When he gets too much to drink, he isn't himself. It's a wonder he hasn't killed somebody before this."

"I doubt if a jury will be too hard on him," Reed said, trying to find something comforting to say.

"It's that gunman," Nettie said angrily. "If he hadn't come to town, none of this would have happened."

Reed couldn't argue with that. If Venango hadn't been in town, Yancey wouldn't have been bragging about how he could gun him down, and he wouldn't have had a gun with him in the alley.

"Do you still want to go to the party?" Reed asked Martha.

"Of course she does," Nettie said quickly before Martha could answer. "This is not going to spoil her evening."

Seeing Martha's agreement, Reed hurried over to the hotel. Some of the townspeople were heading toward Foster's already. Reed quickly shaved and changed into his best clothes.

Martha was ready when he called back at Glee's a few minutes later. She hesitated, though, when Reed suggested they should be on their way.

"Don't you want me to stay with you, Nettie?" she asked.

Nettie shook her head. "You go on to that party. Staying here with me wouldn't help one bit. I've got the kids with me. I'll be all right."

Reed admired Nettie's inner strength. He had known she was strong, or she couldn't have carried on all these years since Yancey had become the town drunk. But it had never shown up as clearly as it did now.

There were buggies and spring wagons and a rack full of saddle horses at Foster's when Reed and

Martha turned up the long walk to the house. It was going to be the biggest social event the town had ever seen.

Inside, Reed looked around at the crowd. He was surprised to see Cal and Clara McBean. Clara still had a purple bruise on her face, and Cal was so weak that he hung into a chair or leaned against the wall most of the time.

"Why did they come?" Martha asked. "They can't have much fun, the way they must feel."

"You're right," Reed agreed. He moved over to the McBeans. "How are you feeling?" he asked Cal.

"Weaker than a sick cat," McBean admitted. "But I'm strong enough to take care of that gunman when he gets here."

Reed saw then that McBean was armed. He didn't doubt that Clara had a gun hidden somewhere in her clothing, too.

"This is no shooting gallery," Reed warned.

"I've got a score to settle with Venango," McBean said. "I figure I'll get my chance at this party—if that gunman isn't too yellow to show up. Nobody else will get hurt."

Reed looked around. Venango wasn't there. He hadn't made any effort to be sociable before, why should he now? Reed was so sure that Johnny Venango wouldn't come to the party that he decided to let the McBeans alone. They wouldn't bother anybody else.

Reed guided Martha through the crowd, greeting everyone. With the exception of the Ortegas, Glees, Venango and Levi Wakefield, everyone seemed to be there. Owen Foster was trying to be friendly, but Reed could see it was a terrific strain. He could imagine how relieved Foster would be when the night was over.

Aleta Foster, on the other hand, was in her glory. She had more stylish things on display than had ever been seen in Rimfire before, and she was reveling in the gasps of delight and admiration coming from the guests.

Reed watched Foster moving around nervously, staying close to the west wall of the big room where the punch bowl was sitting. Reed guessed that the door just behind him probably opened into the room where Foster's safe was.

Three musicians, who had driven into Rimfire in their private coach, now started playing. It was a type of music most of the people there had never heard before, but they made a gallant effort to dance to it.

Reed guided Martha out onto the floor with the others. Before the third dance was over, Tolly came over to cut in. Reed refused to step out and nudged Tolly back toward the wall.

"You'd better save that for Johnny Venango," Tolly warned. "He's out to get you tonight, and he'll do it."

"If you could run as fast as your tongue does, nobody could keep up with you," Reed said. "I told you to leave Martha alone. Don't butt in again."

For a moment, Reed thought Tolly was going to force the issue right there. He didn't want to break up the party with a fight, but he had no intention of backing off. Tolly, however, seemed to think better of it and turned back to the wall.

"I won't ruin Venango's fun," he said.

"What does he mean?" Martha whispered worriedly.

"He's just blowing," Reed said. He looked around. "Do you see the McBeans?"

Reed's eyes raced over the crowd. Burkley

Belling had just come through the door, but the McBeans were not in sight. Maybe they were just not feeling up to staying at the party. That would be understandable. Or maybe they had grown tired of waiting for Johnny Venango to show up and had gone after him. Reed had seen the desperation and fury on their faces when he had talked to them.

Two minutes later, at the end of the dance, Reed noticed that Tolly was no longer in sight. At least Martha would not be bothered by him for the moment. Then Reed saw Emory Larkin moving toward the door. Suspicion nudged him. He could think of a couple of reasons the McBeans had left, but no logical reason for Tolly and Larkin to leave.

"I'm going to have to check on things in town, Martha," Reed said casually. "I don't see Tolly around. Will you be all right?"

"Of course," Martha said, laughing. Then her face sobered. "But you be careful. Maybe Tolly knows something about Venango you don't."

"I doubt it," Reed said.

He hurried toward the door. Martha's concern made him wonder if Tolly's disappearance had just been a ruse to get Reed outside where Venango could get at him. Or maybe Tolly himself would be waiting to ambush him, then lay the blame on Venango.

Reed left Foster's cautiously, watching every dark corner. He walked quickly to his office.

"Things quiet?" he asked.

"As still as a graveyard," Wakefield said.

"You haven't seen the McBeans? Or Tolly or Larkin?"

Wakefield showed surprise. "I haven't been looking for anybody coming from the party. I've kept an eye on the hotel and bank. Nothing stirring

123

either place."

"Why don't you go up to the party for a few minutes? I'll watch things here."

Wakefield nodded. "I won't be gone more than a few minutes. You take care."

Reed nodded and looked over at the hotel. There was a light swinging from the roof of the veranda, and by its illumination, Reed saw Johnny Venango get up and go inside. Apparently he had been sitting on the porch watching the town go to the party. But he obviously had no intention of going himself.

Standing in the doorway, Reed looked up and down the street. Suddenly he tensed. He was sure he had seen Tolly King duck into the alley down by the blacksmith shop. If Tolly was down there now, some kind of mischief was afoot.

CHAPTER XV

Tolly King ducked back behind the blacksmith shop, hoping that Reed Coleman hadn't seen him.

What was Reed doing down here, anyway? He had been at the party when Tolly had left, and Tolly had been sure he would stay as long as Martha did. But he was back in town, and that could cause some complications. He probably wouldn't stay long, though. He'd soon get back to Martha.

Tolly ran on down the alley behind the blacksmith shop. Ellis' house behind the shop was dark. Tolly remembered seeing the Ellis family, kids and all, at the party. At his own house just across from the livery barn, he paused. Stealing a glance up the street, he saw that the marshal was gone from the doorway of his office. The whole street was dark now, except for the lights on the hotel veranda and on the porch of the marshal's office. Still, there was enough light from the sliver of a moon to reveal any movement along the street to anyone watching for it. That was what worried Tolly. Reed might have seen him step out from the blacksmith shop. The moon would soon set, and it would be totally dark, but he couldn't wait.

Sure that the street was empty, Tolly dodged across the street to the barn. He'd get the horses ready just in case he and Larkin stumbled into trouble getting the money from the bank and had to make a run for it. He had thought of turning all the saddled horses up at Foster's place loose so no one could possibly pursue them. But that would be a dead giveaway that something was afoot. And Larkin had said they wanted to pull this off without anyone even suspecting what was going on. So he'd had to let the horses alone.

He'd had the foresight earlier this afternoon to let most of the horses out into the corral. He'd kept Emory Larkin's horse in the barn along with the two best ones that Belling had put there for Tolly to hire out.

Putting the saddles on the three horses, he thought about how furious Larkin would be if he could see him saddling that third horse right now. If they had to run, Tolly figured on taking Martha with him if he could.

Making sure the horses were ready, he went to the front of the barn again. Every horse put up at the barn except these three were outside now. All Tolly needed to do was open the corral gate, and there wouldn't be a horse left for anyone to ride. There was no one in the street, so Tolly dodged across to his house, then made his way up the alley behind his house and the blacksmith shop. At the rear of the bank, he stopped. Larkin was supposed to be there now.

"Over here," a voice called softly.

Tolly moved over to the deep shadows against the rear wall of the bank. Larkin was there.

"Got the horses ready?"

"Sure have," Tolly whispered. "Let's get the money."

Larkin glanced up at the windows on the south side of the hotel across the street. "I sure hope Belling stays at that party."

"He will," Tolly said confidently. "He should be pretty well convinced by now that nothing is going to happen to his precious money. He's been in town since yesterday evening, and nothing has happened. He likes parties, too."

Larkin moved over to the rear window, pushed a screwdriver under it and pried. The window complained with little squeals as it slid up the seldom used grooves. Tolly doubted if this rear window was opened often even on hot days.

Larkin seemed concerned that the squeals might be heard, but Tolly shrugged it off. There was nobody in the hotel except Venango. And he was surely asleep now. Everybody else in town was at the party.

"Go up to the corner of the bank and keep an eye on the street while I work on that safe," Larkin ordered. "If anybody shows up, you warn me quick."

"Sure will," Tolly said.

He thought of going along the street between the hotel and the bank, but decided against that. There was always the chance that Venango wasn't asleep. He'd rather have anybody see him than Venango. The gunman might not shoot him down right there, but he'd catch up with him later and take the money.

Tolly had been at the front corner of the bank peering into the street for what seemed like an hour when he heard an oath inside. Something had gone wrong. He waited a moment, and when he didn't hear voices or a scuffle, he decided that Larkin had not been discovered but that something else was wrong.

Leaving his post, Tolly ran back along the bank and around to the rear window. He heard Larkin shuffling around inside and saw the candle he'd been using for a light. The candle was shielded so that no light could reach the front window.

Tolly climbed through the window. "What's wrong?" he whispered to Larkin.

Larkin wheeled. "There's no money in this safe. Somebody has already cleaned it out."

"Venango!" Tolly said, disappointment making him physically sick.

But before he could even consider what they could do about it, glass shattered at the side window in the bank, and Burkley Belling's voice cut through the darkness.

"Don't move, or I'll gun you down where you stand!"

Larkin dived to one side, clawing for his gun. The gun at the window roared. Tolly took advantage of that instant to leap toward the rear window. He glanced back to see Larkin crumpled in a heap against the wall, the candle still sputtering only inches away.

"There's no money here," Larkin shouted. "Venango got it."

Then Larkin started shooting, and the gun at the window opened up again. While the duel was going on between Belling and Larkin, Tolly scrambled through the rear window and raced down the alley toward his house. He didn't think Belling had seen him. He'd been far enough away from Larkin so that the light from the candle wouldn't have reached him.

The shooting in the bank continued, and Tolly dodged across the street to the barn. In just a minute that shooting would bring everybody from the party. He thought of getting his horse and racing out of town. But then he remembered that Larkin had said that running away would be considered positive proof that they had committed the crime.

Belling hadn't seen him, and Tolly was sure that Larkin wouldn't tell on him. In fact, he doubted if Larkin was alive now. He'd been hit pretty hard by that first bullet, judging from the way he had fallen. And there had been a lot of shooting after that.

Chances were good that Tolly was in the clear. He could stay in town, and no one would suspect he was in on the bank robbery. But something more important had suddenly occurred to Tolly. Johnny Venango surely hadn't taken that money from the bank. He wouldn't have had half as good a chance to take it as Tolly and Larkin had had. So what had happened to it?

Tolly remembered seeing Foster make three or four trips from the bank to his home that afternoon about closing time. Foster must have taken that money home with him where he could watch it. So all Tolly had to do was lie low till after the party broke up, then go to Foster's and make him cough up the money. He'd have the whole thing for himself, too. He wouldn't have to split with anybody.

Up the street, he heard people yelling, asking questions and running along the walks. Stepping to the door, he saw them streaming down from Foster's. He wasn't going to have to wait for the party at Foster's to break up. That shooting had taken care of that.

Stripping the saddle from Larkin's horse, he turned him into the corral. He'd need a sack to carry the money. He ran to the oats bin to find an empty sack. But there wasn't any. He'd let Ed Daisey have all his empty sacks for something he wanted to store in the grocery. There was one sack half full of oats. He'd opened it just yesterday.

Dumping the oats out in a heap, he took the sack and ran to the back door. Nobody would come to the barn, he was sure. Out in the corral, he ran to the gate and opened it. He wouldn't encourage the horses to go out. But if anybody tried to catch one of them, the horses would find that open gate and thunder out and across the creek where nobody could catch them.

Turning up the alley, he ran to the north. By the time he had reached the lumber yard, most of the noise was behind him as people from the party swarmed around the bank, trying to find out what had happened.

At the north end of the lumber yard, Tolly crouched in the shadows and waited until he was certain there was no one left at the party. Lights were still blazing all over Foster's house.

Crossing the street, he ran over the new grass to the house. There he paused, panting from his run. He was sure no one had seen him. Leaning against the wall, he listened. The windows were open, and he could hear someone moving around inside.

"If it's the bank that's been robbed, I don't know why you're not down there to see about it," Aleta Foster called from the kitchen in one end of the house.

"There's nothing I could do if I was down there,"

129

Owen Foster called back from the main room where the party had been. "That's a job for the marshal."

Tolly grinned and tried to calm his breathing. That exchange had told him a lot. Everybody had left the party, and Mrs. Foster was already taking things to the kitchen to start washing dishes. Foster was still in the party room, and he wasn't worried about his bank being robbed. If he didn't know where the money was, he'd be out of his mind with worry now. So the money was there, just as Tolly had guessed.

Tolly moved over to the door. He'd just walk in and demand the money.

Pulling his gun and carrying the sack in his left hand, Tolly stepped through the door, which was still open to let in more of the cool evening air. He whipped the gun around to aim directly at the startled banker. Foster was too surprised to say a word, and Tolly took advantage of that.

"Not a peep out of you, Foster, if you want to live," he said softly. He tossed the sack to him. "Put the bank money in that."

"I don't have the bank money," Foster said, trying to sound convincing.

"You'd better have," Tolly said softly. "You're going to die if you don't fill that sack with money."

"But the money is in the bank."

"You know that's a lie," Tolly said, moving closer to the banker. "I'm going to give you just one minute to fill that sack."

"But—"

Tolly cocked the gun. Foster's eyes bulged, and he took the sack, blubbering like a baby as he moved into the next room. Tolly followed him, his gun in the banker's back.

Foster moved a big overstuffed chair, and there,

130

built into the wall at floor level, was a huge safe, almost as big as the one down at the bank. Foster crouched and began turning the knob.

"I can't remember the combination," he said.

"You've got just thirty seconds left to remember it," Tolly warned. "Don't think for a second I won't shoot. It will be your leg first, then your arm, then your belly. If you don't get that money for me, you're going to die slow."

Foster whimpered again and turned back to the dial. In a few seconds, the big door swung open. Tolly saw three big canvas sacks with a little money and some jewelry outside the sacks. The bank money was in the sacks, Tolly knew, and that was enough for him.

"Put those canvas bags in the sack," he ordered.

As the banker complied, Tolly considered what to do with Foster. Mrs. Foster was still banging away in the kitchen. Nobody but the banker knew he had taken the money.

As Foster turned to hand the oats sack to Tolly, Tolly brought the gun down hard on Foster's head. Foster slumped over without a sound. That should be just as effective as a bullet, Tolly thought, and there hadn't been any noise. He grabbed the oats sack and hurried back into the other room. Mrs. Foster was still in the kitchen. He ran out the front door and across the big lawn.

Behind him, he heard Mrs. Foster yell something to her husband. When he didn't answer, she'd probably go to see why. Then she'd know what had happened, but she wouldn't know who had done it. Nobody would know. Tolly had made a clean getaway.

He ran across the street and behind the lumber yard. He found the sack heavier than he had

131

expected and decided there must be quite a bit of gold as well as paper money. He'd have enough to last him and Martha for years, maybe the rest of their lives.

Running down the alley, he crossed the side street to the rear of Glee's dress shop. There he stopped, breathing hard. His horses were ready. All he needed was Martha, and he could leave the town forever.

There was a light in the corner bedroom, and he moved up to the open window and looked inside. Martha was there. His luck was holding perfectly; this was certainly his night.

Martha was sitting in front of the bureau with her back to the open window. Apparently she hadn't been home from the party long, because she hadn't undressed for bed yet.

Cautiously, Tolly slipped over the window sill. He had to keep Martha from making any fuss. Nettie Glee and the children must be in the other part of the house.

He was within a step of Martha before she became aware of his presence and spun around on the stool where she was sitting. He saw the startled look on her face and read the intake of breath as the beginning of a scream. Reaching over, he clamped a hand over her mouth.

"You won't scream, will you?" he whispered.

She stared at him and finally shook her head. He took his hand away.

"I came to show you something," he said. He dropped the oats sack on the floor. "I've got enough money in there to last us a lifetime. The horses are saddled in the barn. So get into something comfortable for riding, and we'll get going."

"Going?" Martha asked incredulously. "Where?"

"Doesn't make much difference where. We'll be

together, and we'll have all the money we want." He stared at her. "Well, get moving. We can't sit around here till they find out what has happened."

"You're out of your mind!" Martha exclaimed. "That's the bank money you've stolen."

Tolly grinned. She might as well know now how clever he was. "Old Foster thought he was too smart for everybody. He took the money to his house. But I figured it out. Now we've got it all. Let's go."

"I'm not going anywhere with you!" Martha said, anger replacing the surprise on her face.

He frowned. For the first time, he realized that maybe it was going to take more than money to bring Martha to him. "There's lots of money here," he said. "I'll buy you anything you want."

"I don't want anything to do with that money or you. Now get out of here!"

Tolly stared at Martha. He had imagined all kinds of surprised reactions from her when she saw he had so much money. But not once had he even considered the possibility that she would refuse to go with him. He was a rich man now.

"You can have everything you want," he said desperately.

"I just want you out of here immediately!" Martha said. Her voice rising.

That rise in voice prodded him into a decision. He couldn't understand her, but that wasn't important now. He didn't dare leave her there to tell everyone who had killed Foster and taken his money. Whether she wanted to go or not, he had to take her with him. He couldn't kill Martha; at least, not unless he had to.

With a sudden move, Tolly whipped an arm around Martha, clamping a hand over her mouth so she couldn't scream. The way she was acting, she just might try to call for help.

"Come on," he snapped. "You're going with me."

Dragging her off the stool, he pulled her toward the window. She struggled, and he realized she was much stronger than he had ever imagined a little woman could be. But he was strong, too, and he used that strength now to pull her to the window.

He found it difficult to climb out of the window, dragging both the oats sack and Martha without letting her scream. Once in the alley, he started toward the rear of the livery barn, over a block away. They'd never catch him now.

CHAPTER XVI

Reed was back in his office when he heard the first shot down at the bank. He had been thinking of going back to the party. He didn't like to be away from Martha so long. Tolly might return to the party, and he didn't seem to have gumption enough to take no for an answer.

Reed left the office at a run. Even as he sprinted down the middle of the street toward the bank, he thought that whoever was trying to rob the bank was in for a surprise. He was convinced that Foster had taken most of the money, maybe all of it, to his house that afternoon.

More shots came from the bank, and Reed saw the blaze of the gun at the side window on the street between the hotel and the bank. Panting, he stopped beside the window, his gun in his hand. The light was dim, but he saw that the man at the window was Burkley Belling.

"Who's in there?" Reed demanded.

"I don't know," Belling said. "Sounded like

134

Emory Larkin. He yelled that Venango had already robbed the bank."

"Has he been shooting at you?"

"He sure has," Belling said. "He's not far from that candle in there. He must have been using the candle to see to open the safe."

Reed looked through the window. The safe door was open, and there was a man sprawled on the floor not far from the safe. The candle was sputtering on the floor two feet from him.

Reed could see that Belling had no intention of pushing his luck by going into the bank. But Reed had to find out if the man was alive and just what had happened. Breaking out the splinters of glass still clinging to the window frame, he carefully stepped through, his gun on the unmoving figure on the floor.

Once inside, he moved quickly to the man and touched him. He didn't stir. Stooping, Reed felt for the man's pulse. There was none. Rolling him over, he saw that it was Larkin.

He picked up the candle and looked in the safe. Not much there. Certainly all the big money was gone. There was no sign of any money near the safe. Reed wasn't surprised; he was sure the money was up in Foster's house.

"Who is it?" Belling asked from the window. "Is he dead?"

"It's Larkin, and he is dead. There's no money here, either."

"Then he was telling the truth," Belling said. "Venango did beat him to it."

Reed climbed back through the broken window. People were swarming down the street from the direction of Foster's, apparently attracted by the shots.

"What makes you think Venango took the money?"

"Who else in this town would rob the bank?" Belling said. "I'm going after that gunman."

"Now hold on," Reed warned. "In the first place, if Venango did get the money, which I doubt, he isn't going to let anybody take it away from him. In the second place, it's my job as marshal to find out who got the money."

"You've been pussy-footing around that gunman ever since he got here," Belling snapped. "You'll find some excuse to let him go again."

"I'll check first to see if his horse is gone from the barn," Reed said. "If he hasn't left town, we can corral him easy enough. In the meantime, I don't want you going off half cocked and getting yourself killed."

"I'm going to get my money back," Belling said.

"You'll get it back," Reed said confidently. "But if you're dead, you're not going to enjoy it much."

Belling nodded reluctantly, and Reed turned toward the street. It was as near to a promise that Belling wouldn't go after Venango alone as Reed was going to get from him.

In the street, Reed turned toward the livery barn. Venango had stabled his horse there. If it was there now, that would mean that the gunman was still in town. Reed was sure that Venango was right up there in his hotel room. But if he told Belling that, he'd ask more questions, and Reed would have to tell him that he suspected Foster of taking the bank money home with him. If he was guessing wrong, he'd never be able to explain his error.

The barn was dark except for the lantern hanging out in front. It always hung there until late each night. Cautiously, Reed pushed open the front door

136

and stepped inside. He wasn't sure what to expect. He recalled seeing Emory Larkin and Tolly King together today. That could mean something, or it could mean nothing. But since Larkin had been killed robbing the bank, there was a possibility that Tolly was involved in the robbery, too.

Reed listened attentively for a moment inside the barn, but all he heard was the stamping of a horse's foot. Striking a match, he located the lantern that hung on a wire that stretched the length of the barn. Lighting the wick, he lowered the globe and slid the lantern along the wire, looking into each stall as he passed.

He was surprised to find only two horses in the barn, both saddled. He recognized the horses as two of the best animals belonging to the barn. Maybe Larkin and Tolly planned to take these two fast horses to escape, leaving Larkin's horse there.

Reed stepped to the back door and peered out into the corral. Several horses were there, and one of those nearest the barn was Venango's horse. So the gunman was still in town, just as Reed had thought.

Turning back into the barn, he slid the lantern along the wire to the front. If Larkin and Tolly were in this together, where was Tolly now? And where had he been when Belling had gunned down Larkin?

His eye fell on the pile of oats just outside the oats bin. Why would Tolly spill so many oats? And all in a neat pile? Suddenly it all began to drop into place. He jerked open the oats bin. The oats had been brought to the barn in sacks, and there were no empty sacks in the bin. Tolly had needed an empty sack. And it took Reed only a moment to know what he wanted it for.

Blowing out the lantern, Reed hurried to the front door and into the street. Tolly must have figured the same thing he had—that Foster had taken the money home with him that afternoon. Now that he thought of it, Reed hadn't seen Foster in the crowd of people who had swarmed down from the party. If that money had been in the bank, Foster would have been the first one down there when the shooting started.

Foster was probably still home. If so, it proved beyond a doubt that the bank's money was there, too. And probably Tolly was on his way up there right now. Or maybe he was already there. Reed started toward the north end of town.

People were still milling around in the street, and Belling was the center of the questions. Reed hurried past, answering very briefly any questions that were tossed at him. Apparently no one else had even guessed that Foster had taken the money home with him.

By the time Reed reached the church, he had begun to run. If he was guessing right, he'd have to hurry to prevent Tolly from breaking into the Foster home and getting the money.

The lights were still blazing in Foster's house when he went past Levi Wakefield's place and turned onto the wide lawn. He heard something then, half sob and half scream, that sent him sprinting for the house. He realized that he couldn't have heard that sound before because of the noise being made by the milling crowd back in the street.

He shoved open the door into the big room where the party had been held. Mrs. Foster was in the next room, on her knees beside her husband. Reed knelt beside her.

"When did this happen?" Reed asked, not bothering to ask who or what. He was sure he knew the answers to both questions.

138

"I don't know. I was washing dishes in the kitchen." Mrs. Foster stifled another sob. "I called to Owen. When he didn't answer, I came to see why, and I found him like this."

Reed felt for the banker's pulse. It was there, but not too strong. "He's alive," he said. "I'll send Dr. Singer up here right away. Did you see anyone?"

Mrs. Foster shook her head. "It couldn't have happened more than five minutes ago. Owen was talking to me then."

Reed looked past the big chair to the open safe behind it. "They were after the money."

Mrs. Foster shook her head. "My jewels are there. And we didn't have much money here."

"He had the bank money here," Reed said. "I'll send the doc up."

He ran across the big room and out the door. He had to get back to the barn before Tolly got there. As he was passing the church, he saw the swarm of people coming up the street toward him. There was no avoiding them. Burkley Belling was in the lead, and he saw Cal McBean and his wife close behind him.

"What did you find out?" Belling demanded as soon as he was close enough to make Reed hear. "Is Venango gone?"

"No," Reed said. "His horse is still here. He had nothing to do with the bank robbery."

"If he's still here, he had something to do with it," McBean said. "I say we should storm that hotel and drag him out and hang him."

"You're too weak to hang a cat," Reed said in disgust.

"I'm not," Clara McBean said. "I'll help hang him."

"They've got the right idea," Belling said.

139

"Now you hold on," Reed shouted loud enough for those behind Belling and the McBeans to hear. "I think I know who robbed the bank, and I'm after him now. Just you hold your horses till I get back. Is that clear?"

"We're not sitting around while Venango gets away," Belling shouted.

"He's not going anywhere. If you make sure he doesn't get his horse, you know he'll stay in town."

A few heads behind Belling nodded. Belling reluctantly agreed.

"We'll give you ten minutes," he said. "If you haven't got the robber by then, we'll get him for you. And we won't have to ask who he is, either."

Satisfied that was all he was going to get out of Belling, Reed located Dr. Singer and sent him to Foster's. He had already been delayed longer than he liked. He hurried on and was in front of Nettie Glee's dress shop when he heard a woman scream in the alley behind. Wheeling into the passageway between Glee's house and his own office, he ran to the alley.

It was dark between the buildings and not much lighter in the alley behind them. But the instant he came out into the alley, a shot split the darkness. Reed dived backward as the bullet thudded into the corner of the jail.

He didn't know who had shot at him, for he hadn't seen anyone. But he had located the source of the shot. The gunman was down the alley a short distance, about even with the harness shop.

Standing there, breathing hard, Reed quickly pieced things together. It had to be Tolly out there. He'd have the bank money and probably Martha. Knowing his infatuation with Martha and his insane idea that Martha would go anywhere with him, Reed

140

jumped to the conclusion that he had stopped to get her. With the money and Martha, he'd have everything he wanted. That could explain the other saddled horse down in the barn. It would also explain the scream, because Martha would object to being dragged off by Tolly.

Men came running into the passageway between the harness shop and the marshal's office. Others came down between the harness shop and the drugstore. A few came up behind Reed, where he stopped them.

"Don't anybody shoot!" Reed shouted. "He's got Martha."

"Who is it? Venango?"

Somebody came down by the drugstore, swinging a lantern. As the dim flickering light hit the alley, it revealed Tolly standing there with a gun in his hand, holding Martha in front of him.

"If you want her to live, you'd better stay right where you are!" Tolly shouted. "If anybody steps into the alley, she gets shot." Tolly was whipping his head back and forth to look at everybody peering out of the darkness toward him. He had the wild desperate look of a cornered animal.

Somebody brought another lantern down the passageway on the other side of the jail. It threw more light into the alley. Levi Wakefield came up behind Reed.

"I'm going down to the end of the alley," he said softly to Reed. "Got to keep him from getting to the barn. I might be able to distract his attention, too."

Reed nodded. "Good idea. I'll be ready. Don't expose yourself. He'll kill you if he can."

Tolly was getting nervous. He seemed unsure how to proceed. He was safe as long as everything remained a stalemate. But even he must realize that he had to get to his horses soon. The deadlock couldn't last.

Tolly jammed the gun against the side of Martha's head. "I'm leaving here," he shouted. "If anybody makes a false move, she'll die."

"Nobody's doing anything," Reed shouted.

Knowing that Tolly had been crazy enough to think that Martha would gladly go anywhere with him, Reed wasn't sure that he might not be crazy in other respects, too. Certainly he might decide to kill Martha because she wouldn't go willingly with him.

Tolly had moved only a few feet toward the livery barn when Wakefield stepped into the alley down by the saloon.

"Tolly, let her go," he shouted.

Tolly wheeled toward this new threat. As he spun around, he exposed his side to Reed. It gave Reed a small target in the uncertain light from the lanterns. It was a desperate chance, but he doubted if he would get a better one.

Stepping into the alley, he aimed quickly and carefully. He screamed to Martha to drop down as he squeezed the trigger.

Tolly's shot, aimed at Wakefield, went wild as Reed's bullet slammed into him. Martha threw herself sideways, leaving Tolly alone and exposed. As Martha rolled away, two other guns from farther down the alley spewed fire at Tolly.

Tolly was knocked backward into the dust of the alley. Reed was the first one to break away from the buildings and race toward Tolly and Martha.

He stopped first at Martha, who was on her hands and knees. "Are you hurt?"

Martha shook her head. "I'm all right."

Reed turned to Tolly. At first he thought he was dead. He was sprawled on his back, his gun a foot from his outflung fingers. But his eyes were open, and he was conscious.

"You have all the luck," he whispered as Reed bent over him. "I tried to kill you at the river, but I missed." His breath was coming in short gasps. "Tried to get Martha—money from the bank. Missed both."

Dr. Singer appeared out of the darkness, panting from his run from Foster's, and knelt beside Reed. Reed got up, letting the doctor take over. He wouldn't have much luck with Tolly, Reed was sure. Levi Wakefield came running up the alley, and Reed picked up the oats sack of money and handed it to him.

"Watch this," he said. "I've got to stop Belling from making a bigger fool of himself than he already has. He's sure Venango stole his money."

"Better hurry," Wakefield said. "Belling and the McBeans were outside the hotel when I went past a couple of minutes ago."

Reed ran through the narrow alleyway between the drugstore and the harness shop into the street.

At first he didn't see anyone. Then he located Belling over by the side of the hotel, looking up at the veranda as if expecting to see someone come out of the hotel at any second. Reed ran across the street to him.

"We got your money back," Reed said.

Belling turned to stare at Reed. "How? I thought Venango was in the hotel."

"He probably is. Tolly King took it."

Belling's jaw dropped. "Tolly? That ungrateful pup! Was that him doing the shooting over there?"

"He did some of it," Reed said. "You can call off your war with Johnny Venango now. He didn't touch your money."

Belling nodded, as though suddenly realizing this changed everything. "Cal McBean and his wife went in the hotel after Venango," he said. "Cal seems determined to kill that gunman. He won't even give a reason."

Reed leaped up on the end of the veranda. He didn't like the idea of going into the hotel after the McBeans. But somebody had to stop them. If they had any reason to kill Venango, it was a personal one. They could no longer hide behind the excuse that he had robbed the bank.

Before Reed reached the front door, a volley of shots exploded somewhere inside the hotel. Leaping forward, Reed dodged through the doorway. The shots had come from the floor above.

He took the steps two at a time, his gun in his hand. At the top of the stairs, he paused. He could get shot if he charged in recklessly.

"This is the marshal," he shouted. "What happened?"

He heard a woman crying then. But still he waited. Then Venango's voice came from down the hall.

"Back here, Marshal. This scatterbrain tried to kill me."

Reed turned down the dimly lit hallway. He saw them then. Johnny Venango was just outside the door of his room. Cal McBean was sprawled on the floor, and Clara McBean was kneeling beside him, crying.

"Why did he try to kill you?" Reed asked as he reached Venango.

"I don't know," Venango said. "I never saw him till I came to this town."

"Cal was sure that he'd come here to kill him," Clara McBean said between sobs. "Cal filled a prescription years ago that killed several people. The husband of a woman who died swore he would get Cal some day. We thought he had sent Venango to kill Cal."

"I didn't have any choice," Venango said. "He was trying to kill me."

Reed nodded. "I guess what his wife says verifies that. From what I hear, half the people in town think you came here to kill them."

He knelt beside McBean and felt for a pulse. There was none. He lifted Clara McBean to her feet and guided her toward the stairs.

"Come on down," he said over his shoulder. "That crowd over in the alley will be swarming over here. Maybe if you'll tell them why you did come to Rimfire, we can have some peace."

Reed guided Clara McBean down to the front of the hotel. He was aware that Johnny Venango was just behind him. He knew that there could be more trouble. If Venango was really after someone in town, this might give him the opportunity he was looking for. Or perhaps somebody else who, like McBean, was sure that Venango was after him might try to get the gunman first.

As Reed expected, most of the people who had been over in the alley were milling around in front of the hotel now, afraid to go in until they knew what was happening.

Reed led Clara McBean out on the veranda, but Johnny Venango stopped in the shadows just inside the doorway, showing the instincts of a gunman even though he was in the escort of the town marshal.

Reed quickly explained what had happened upstairs in the hotel. "You've been blaming Johnny Venango for everything," he concluded. "Even Mrs.

145

McBean admits that Venango shot Cal in self-defense. And you all know now that he didn't rob the bank."

"What is he here for?" one man demanded.

Reed turned to Venango. "I guess we all want to know that."

"I came to Rimfire," Venango said, barely showing himself in the doorway, "because I thought it was a peaceful town where I could relax and not have to watch my back all the time."

"You didn't come after anybody?" Ed Daisey asked.

"I never saw a soul in this town before I rode in. I had hoped no one here had ever seen or heard of me."

"Nobody had heard of you," Reed said. "They just jumped at conclusions."

"I guess a man can't change from what he is," Venango said wearily. "A gunman has to kill."

Reed nodded agreement. But that applied to more than just the gunman. Looking out at the crowd in front of the hotel and thinking of McBean and Tolly and Foster, he knew that the same rule applied to them. They could hide their true personalities for a long time, but when the blue chips fell on the table, their real natures came out. No one could run away from himself. The town had gotten a good look at the real people who made it. And Reed wasn't sure that anybody there liked what he had seen.

Dr. Singer came through the crowd to Reed. "Tolly is dead," he said. "I saw Owen Foster. He will live, but he told me how he got his money. I reckon that will be a job for you to handle, Marshal. He won't be the big man in Rimfire any longer. He was also sure that Venango had come after him."

Reed sighed and turned to Johnny Venango.

146

"Looks like you can stay in Rimfire in peace now."

Venango shook his head. "I'll be riding on in the morning. A man like me always has to ride on."

Reed stepped down from the porch and worked his way toward Martha at the edge of the crowd. Burkley Belling stopped him.

"I guess we all showed our skunk stripes the last couple of days," he said. "Tolly sure fooled me. I've had about all the trouble I need for a while."

Reed guessed what Belling was getting around to saying. "Are you willing to have me for a neighbor?"

Belling nodded. "Getting that patch of land of yours just ain't worth any more trouble."

Reed watched Belling turn and head for the livery barn, where he had stabled his horse when he'd ridden in yesterday afternoon. He believed Belling. Now that he'd decided not to plague Reed for that land any more, he'd stand by his decision.

Reed moved on to Martha, who was waiting for him.

"We won't have any more trouble now, will we?" she asked.

He grinned. "None whatsoever—unless you balk at letting Levi marry us."

She snuggled under his arm. "No trouble whatsoever," she said.

We hope that you enjoyed reading this
Sagebrush Large Print Western.
If you would like to read more Sagebrush titles,
ask your librarian or contact the Publishers:

United States and Canada

Thomas T. Beeler, *Publisher*
Post Office Box 659
Hampton Falls, New Hampshire 03844-0659
(800) 251-8726

United Kingdom, Eire, and
the Republic of South Africa

Isis Publishing Ltd
7 Centremead
Osney Mead
Oxford OX2 0ES England
(01865) 250333

Australia and New Zealand

Australian Large Print Audio & Video P/L
17 Mohr Street
Tullamarine, Victoria, 3043, Australia
1 800 335 364

A0000106353790